For the Love of It All

Him. Her. They.

MONIKA D. WILLIAMSON

First published by Black Silk Inc. 2021 in the United States.

www.fortheloveofitallbook.com

Designed by The Regal Group.

First edition: 2021

ISBN: 978-0-578-94734-1 (trade paperback)

This book is dedicated to my cousin, Ebony Elis. You always believed in me even when I didn't. Rest in Heaven. I love rainbows now.

To My Imagination: We have fought a hard battle that we never thought we would win, but we did it. Here is to many more stories we have yet to create.

To My Kids and Family: Thank you for the continued support and laughs; you are the best prayer warriors anyone could be blessed with.

To My Readers: Thank you for joining me in this ride I call an urban novella. Sit Back and Enjoy the Ride.

CONTENTS

"Please don't read positive, please don't be positive," I stared down at the digital pregnancy test, sitting on the floor in my upstairs bathroom. "It can't read positive; it just can't." Positive. "What the Fuck? This can't be right," I shouted as I threw the pregnancy test across the bathroom. How in God's name could I be pregnant?

I remember the day my OBGYN told me the news clear as day, sitting in her office seven months ago. "I am sorry to tell you, Meshia, but you won't be able to have any children; the abortions left too much scar tissue." I left that office feeling like my world was just crushed and all from something out of my control.

Just now, when I finally start getting my life back together, life throws in this shit. My phone started ringing Tank's "Heart breaker." I didn't even have to look to know it was Markus. He was the only one that would be calling me besides my best friend, Renee. I let the call go to voicemail as I stared at the pregnancy test, "WTF am I going to do?"

MARKUS

"Positive, we need to talk ASAP" ~*Meshia*

I had been starring at this same message for over an hour and still couldn't believe what it read. How could I let this shit happen? How could I have been so careless? Well, I know how it happened, probably one of those late-night "meetings" I had with Meshia, which ended up with her spread eagle on my desk with my dick buried so far inside of her, you would have thought I was digging for oil. Whenever I was anywhere near Meshia, I lost all common sense that would tell me to put on a condom. Plus, she told me she couldn't get pregnant.

I responded with a text message, "Thought U said U couldn't get Prego."

"Obviously , the doctors were wrong" ~ *Meshia*

"Oh, so now you trying to be a smart ass... U sure it's mine?"

"U was up in it, wasn't you" ~*Meshia*

"Yea, so could every other dude in the metroplex."

"FUCK you, Mark!" ~*Meshia*

"Yea, that's what got us in this mess; hit me when you find out if it's mine." I tossed my phone across my desk.

The truth is I knew Meshia wasn't fucking anyone else; she wasn't that type. A part of me wished she was because the only thing I could think about was how in the hell I was going to explain this shit to Tracie.

"UGH, Girl, I don't know how you can sit up in here with no AC on," my best friend Nichole said while walking into my living room, taking a seat on the couch. "Girl, when you are seven months pregnant with twins, you will understand," I said while rubbing my hands over my swollen belly.

"Ouch, Aweeee," I felt two lower kicks to my ribs that caused me to roll onto my side.

"These babies better come out playing basketball like their daddy because they are tearing up my inside," I said, getting up from the floor and walking towards the kitchen for some iced tea." Let's hope there are nothing like their father," Nichole said under her breath.

I stopped halfway down the hall and turned back to her. "AND what is that supposed to mean," walking back to the couch with my hands folded across my chest. "Nothing, T. I am just saying that Markus isn't the best role model for you to want your kids to be like," Nichole said while moving to the other side of the couch, making room for me to sit down.

"HE is their father; HE is the BEST role model for them," I said, turning to look my golden-eyed best friend in the face.

Nichole's eyes twinkled with mischief, with a crooked smile on her face, "U sure about that." Just as I was about to reply, my phone started ringing "First Love" by Avant. "Speaking of my children's FATHER," I said as I picked up the phone and pressed answer," Hey babe."

I was sitting outside in my black charger... "Hey boo, how're my three babies doing?" Tracie giggling. "We are good, babe. When are you coming home?" Leaning back in my driver side seat,

"Awe, babe, I won't be home til late... something came up with one of the producers, and I have to handle it." Tracie said with disappointment, "Awe, babe, you know I was looking forward to us eating together, and you know we were going to put the cribs together tonight."

"Ahh yeah, babe," I said as I watched Meshia walk outside, headed to her car.

"I know, babe. I know. I promise I will make it up to you later." Getting out of my car, walking towards Meshia. Babe, I have to go; I will be home as soon as I can. "

"Okay, babe, I love you." CLICK was the dial tone from Markus hanging up on me. I didn't know whether to be mad or to cry. "Girl, what excuse did he give this time?" Said Nichole, making me remember that I wasn't in my house alone.

I turned around, facing Nichole, trying to put a smile on my face, "Girl, please, he has a meeting to go to." Nichole looked at me with the same face she always does when she knows I am lying. "But girl, carrying these babies is making me sleepy, so I'm going to have to take a rain check on the rest of this girl time." "Yeah, sure, okay girl … I can take a hint, but you're not fooling anyone; I know you want to be alone, so you can cry cause once again, Markus has flaked on you … But I will let you do that in peace... but for real, T you deserve better…," Nichole said as she grabbed her purse and headed towards the door. Turning around before she opened the door and walked out … "Really T you deserve better," and she walked out the door. As I sat down on the couch, one of my boys kicked my belly. I placed my hand on my belly, rubbing the spot where he kicked, with tears rolling down my face, "Your Auntie Nichole is wrong; I don't deserve better" …Then the heavy tears fell as I thought about who Markus was out there fucking now.

MESHIA

"Hey, can we talk?" Markus said. I looked up and saw Markus standing there in an all-black suit; I just stared at him. "Meshia, can we talk," Markus said as he stepped towards me. "Meshia, we needed to talk." I turned around to open the car door, completely ignoring him. I didn't have shit to say to this nigga. Markus grabbed the car door and pulled my hand, pulling me backwards into him... "Come on, Mesh, you know you can't stay mad at me ... look at me," he said as he lowered his head close to my neck, gently brushing the long dark brown hair away from my neck. "Baby, please," he gently whispered before he placed small kisses on the side of my neck. I closed my eyes, savoring the soft, warm lips that I used to think I wouldn't be able to live without... A passing car broke my stance, and I turned around to Markus, and my heart skipped a beat. "Get in "... is all I said as I pushed out of his embrace..." What," Markus said as he tried to regain his composure. "Get in the Car!" I yelled, stepping into the driver's side of my white 2013 Lexus.

"Why, where are we going? We need to talk," Markus said nervously, rushing over to the passenger side of the car.

"Shut up and for once in your life, stop trying to be in control," I said as I tried to hold back the anger and tears that had been threatening to pour out. Reluctantly, Markus got into the car and put on his seat belt... turning to look at me. "Okay, I am in the car, now where are we going?" I turned to look at him with tears rolling down my face, "The Clinic."

MESHIA

As I pulled up into the clinic's parking lot, I could feel the tension in the car. We hadn't said anything the entire ride to each other. Just as I pulled into the parking space, I started to feel light-headed and dizzy. As I began to open my car door, I felt Markus's hand cover mine. "We don't have to do this," Markus said. I turned to look at him and saw tears and stress in his brown eyes. For the first time since he got in the car, I realized that the confident and calm man that I was so in love with wasn't sitting next to me. There sat a man who was nervous and stressed, probably worried about his wife finding out that he had another baby on the way. But I couldn't let myself care because I needed my anger at him to get me through what I was about to do.

"This is what you want; this is what you so rudely express to me, this is what you wanted, to keep your precious little family, so don't you dare sit there and act as if you give two shits about the baby inside my stomach," I said, with tears streaming down my face.

"Meshia I," Markus said quietly.

"Don't say shit, Markus. It doesn't matter; you don't love me and don't care about this baby so let's just get this over with so I can be done with you and this nightmare," I screamed, getting out of the car and slamming the door. Markus sat in the car, silent and not moving. I said, "Get out of the fucking car Markus, get out and let's go kill our baby." Markus still didn't move; he sat there like he was in a trance. I walked over to the passenger side door and yanked it open … "Markus," I said… "I Love You," Markus said, still sitting still… "What did you say?" I said, taking a step back. "I said, I love you, Meshia Young," Markus said as he got out of the car and grabbed me in a tight hug. "I said, I love you, Meshia, and I can't let you kill my baby. I love you, and I can't let you go. I just can't," Markus said as he held me tighter with tears coming down his face. I tried to pull out of his grasps, but he just held me tighter and buried his face in my neck …"Let me go, Markus, let me go!" … I screamed. He finally loosed his grip enough for me to pull away, and I started walking towards the front door of the clinic." "Meshia, did you just hear me? I said, I love you, and I want our baby," Markus said as he ran to block the front door… "You don't love me, Markus, you love Tracie, and your twins are on the way," I said, not looking him in his eyes, afraid that I would actually find love staring back at me. "Look at me, Meshia," Markus said …I moved my head towards the highway… "Dammit, look at me," Markus yelled, pulling my head… so I was forced to look at him… "I said I love you, and I mean that. I just need some time," Markus said before pulling my lips to his and engulfing me in an embrace. I pulled back and saw lust, not love staring back at me.

I turned over; just as I heard the garage door open, 3:45 am, the alarm clock read. (Kick one...) "Damn, little ones, give mommy a break," I whispered to myself as I sat up in the bed, wanting to see his face when he walked in to lie to me. I can hear him in the kitchen, probably looking for the plate that I usually leave him every night. As I snapped on the side table light on my nightstand, Kick 2. This one was a little harder than the next. This kick made me rub my belly, "Okay, boys calm down; daddy's finally home," I finished saying just as the door to the bedroom opened... With a shocked look on his face, Markus: "Oh, hey babe, uhh what are you doing up? I thought you would be asleep." "I just woke up; your sons won't let me sleep; you know that they are only still when you're here, sleep next to me," I said as I got up and approached him and tried to wrap my arms around his neck for a hug. But Markus pushed my arms away, "Hey babe, I stink; I smell like a studio. Let me go hit the shower. Go back to bed; I'll be there soon." "Studio, huh, ok, I'll join you... I could use a hot shower to calm these boys." "UHHH, no, that's okay, I'm good," Markus said as he quickly walked past me and into the bathroom, closing and locking the door. I walked over to the door and banged, "Markus are you kidding me? When have you ever turned me down to join you" Really...."T, go back to bed...? I'll be out soon," Markus said with the shower turned on. I stood outside the bathroom door with my back to it, using it as support. I then felt two hard kicks and a sharp pain ripple through the right side of my stomach... "Hey hey, boys, calm down in there," I said as I rubbed the spot where the pain was coming from. Kick kick, more pain... this time sharper and stronger than the last.

I heard Markus's phone ring and the shower door open. "Hello .... Yes, Okay.... I told you I would tell her" .... I heard Markus say to someone on his phone. Kick Kick, three more shots of pain rippled through my stomach, each one stronger than the last. "Don't be like that; I told you I was coming back... shit, she is seven months ... come on, yes... okay, I WILL TELL HER TONIGHT." Just as I reached for the door handle to knock on the door, another pain rippled through my stomach, and I felt a gush of something hot between my legs. "M.... A. R." I tried to call out and knock on the door while reaching down to reach under my legs. "M.... A... R," I said, pulling my hands back and seeing it covered in mucus and bright red blood. Just as another sharp pain made me light-headed and hurt so bad, it sent tears to my eyes. "Markus," I whispered, just as I felt my legs give out and my body beginning to fall to the floor. I tried to brace myself for the fall, but another sharp pain rolled through my stomach and to my back. Just before I blacked out, I heard Markus open the back-room door and say... "Okay, Meshia, I love you too."

"Where is he... damn," I said as I looked at my alarm clock, and it read 3:45 am. I looked around at my condo living room; I guess I must have fallen asleep on the couch waiting for him. I looked down at my phone to see if I had any missed calls from him ... Only thing staring back at me was the picture of him and me from our trip to Las Vegas two months ago. I walked over to my living room window, which gave me a breath-taking view of downtown Dallas.... Remembering the last phone conversation, I had with Markus earlier in the evening. I had called him because I was feeling unsure. "Are you sure you are coming back for good? Markus" "Hello yes... I told you I would tell her" ..."Are you sure? If you are just saying that so that you can string me along, I swear Markus I will...." Markus: "Don't be like that; I told you I was coming back... shit, she is seven months." Me: "And I am pregnant too... do you love me? Tell her!"

Markus: "Calm Down, Meshia. I said, okay, I WILL TELL HER TONIGHT!"

Me: "Okay, babe, hurry, I miss you.

Markus: "I'll be there soon."

I walked over to my living room window, which gave me a breath-taking view of downtown Dallas...

"Fuck, Markus, where are you?"

MARKUS

"How did I let this happen? Shit, how the hell did I even get in this situation. Please, God, let T and my boys be okay. Please God... I will do right by them if you let them be okay. Please God," I prayed as I sat in the waiting room at Dallas Presbyterian Hospital, the Women's Ward. My mind kept replaying what had happened in the last few hours; I knew I had hurt Tracie when I told her I didn't want her company in the shower; I had never denied her before. I just couldn't sleep with her, knowing I had just been up inside Meshia. Shit Meshia, I was supposed to be there hours ago. Just as I pulled out my phone, Tracie's mom and dad walked up. Just as I stood up to greet them, Mrs. Ellis rushed into my arms. "Oh God, Markus, what did they say ... how is my baby? What happened," Mrs. Ellis asked with tears down her face.

"Morgan, calm down; I am sure they are doing the best they can for her and the boys," Mr. Ellis said as he extended his hand for a handshake. Just as I was about to respond, Tracie's doctor, Dr. Allen, who looked about 25, came walking into the waiting room with a stern face. "Mr. Damon, your wife has lost a lot of blood during the surgery; she is in a critical condition. We are doing everything we can for her." "Surgery, what. Wait... why?" I asked with a confused look.

"Oh my God, my baby," Mrs. Ellis cried out, placing her head on her husband's shoulder.

"It's going to be okay, Morgan ... calm down, baby, let the doctor finish.... What is the bleeding from?" Mr. Ellis asked.

"Your daughter had a medical condition called pre-eclampsia, which is very common in first-time mothers, though sometimes it can go undetected when dealing with multiple births. We are doing everything we can for her," Dr. Allen replied.

"And the boys, how are the boys?" I said, barely able to get out the words. Dr. Allen took a deep breath," Mr. Damon, both boys, although small, are doing well in the neonatal unit.

I fell to my knees as I realized what he had just told me. "Thank you, God, for saving my boys; please bring Tracie back to me. I promise to do right by her. I promise, please just let her live, I pleaded mentally. I tried to speak, but nothing came out as Dr. Allen and a nurse rushed over to me. I could hear Tracie's mom hollering and whaling behind me as I tried to compose myself. I looked up at Dr. Allen through my tear-stained eyes, "I, I, I want to see them," I said as I stood on my feet. "I want to see my boys." "Of course, Mr. Damon, this way to the NICU." "Go ahead, son; we will wait right here for the nurse to tell us about Tracie. Go see our grandchildren," Mr. Ellis said as he comforted his wife with tears in his eyes. As I slowly followed Dr. Allen down the hall, I felt my cell phone vibrate in my pants pocket. I took it out, and the message read, "Where are you? Love Meshia." I looked back at the room that held my infant sons and then back at my phone, then back at my boys and the phone

again...Dr. Allen called out to me, "Mr. Damon ...are you coming."
I looked at my phone one last time and hit the delete button, and
tossed my phone in the trash, remembering the plea I just made to
God for Tracie's life and said, "Coming, Doc."

Meshia

When I woke up the next morning, I expected to see Markus lying next to me in the bed. I must have been more tired than I thought. The spot next to me was just as empty as my heart felt.

The whole night I had been praying that he had come in while I was sleeping. The reality that he chose her was setting in, and tears began to swell in my eyes as I knew what I had to do. I got out of my bed and grabbed my phone to make the hardest call of my life. One thing Markus knew is I was a woman of my word, and once I said I would do something, I followed through. As I got out of bed, I grabbed my phone to see if I had any missed calls or texts, nothing. The tears were now falling from my eyes as I googled the number I needed. I couldn't believe how stupid I was to believe that Markus would actually leave his pregnant wife for me. "Damn," I said as the ring tone rang twice on the other end of my phone. I fell for someone who wasn't mine and never would be. By the third ring, a wave of nausea hit the bottom of my stomach, forcing me to drop my phone on my bed as I ran to my bathroom with my hand over my mouth. I was throwing up and crying so hard and violently; it felt like my heart was trying to come from my chest, up to my throat, and land right into the toilet. It seemed like forever, but only 15 minutes had passed when I was finally able to move away from the toilet and support myself with both hands on the sink. "Get it together, girl!" I said to myself after a few breaths. I rinsed my mouth out with Listerine and brushed my teeth. I walked back into my bedroom and picked up my phone and hit the same number again. They answered after the first ring this time. "Thank you for calling Planned Parent Hood; how can I help you?" The operator on the other end said. I paused for a bit, wrapping away from the fresh tears that had slipped from my eyes, and spoke, "I need to make another appointment."

8 months later....

Ugh, I knew as soon as I pulled up, at 11:30 am instead of 9:00 am, that Renée was going to be mad and have an attitude. A few months ago, I had agreed to cook at one of her clients' birthday parties, located out in Plano. Heck, I would have been on time had I not overslept and for traffic.

As I got out of my car, I was able to take in the 6-bedroom mansion that had its own recording studio, basketball court, and movie theater; I let out a sigh. "This house is amazing." I walked through the side door where I saw a massive Ice Sculptor in the shape of a T.

"Well, Well, look who finally showed her face?" Renee said as I entered the massive kitchen, which was state of the art. You could tell no expense had been spared. "Renee, you know I wouldn't have been late if it wasn't for that damn traffic on 635. Plus, I knew Jose is more than capable of handling things til I got here," I said as I pulled on my chef jacket. "It wasn't Jose that my client specifically requested for this party, Mesh," Rene said, using the nickname she had given me at the age of 7.

"You're the famous one, so please get to work and do your magic." I rolled my eyes as she walked away. For the next 3 hours, the staff, Jose, and I prepared the 5-course meal and four cakes requested by Renee's client. As I stood over the sink washing my hands, the running water reminded me that I had been holding out on going to the restroom. As I dried my hands and walked towards the living room, I shouted to Jose, "Hey, I'll be right back, go ahead and have the staff get ready to serve the first course." He nodded his head while never looking up from the key lime pie pastries he was icing. Walking quickly through the living room, searching for Renee, to ask her where the bathroom was. I heard her yelling at someone to find out where T was. As I was walking towards Renee's voice, I bumped into a woman dressed in a blood-red halter dress with sea-blue eyes. "Oh, I am so sorry," I started to say, but the woman cut me off, "Bitch, watch where you're walking," and before I could respond, she swung her 26-inch blonde extensions over her shoulder and walked towards the back of the mansion. I stood there about to follow her and snatch her bad extensions off her head and teach her some manners, but my bladder was not going to hold any longer. I ran up the winding staircase that was to my left and threw my chef hat on the table next to it. Taking the stairs two at a time, I made it to the top and went to the right, opening six doors before I finally found a bathroom. I barely made it to the bathroom before I would have embarrassed myself. I started thinking about how rude the lady in the red dress was, like who wears a red dress with blonde highlights; that thought made me giggle. I flushed the toilet and washed my hands. While I was drying my hands, I got a glimpse of my reflection. Shit, no wonder that lady looked at me like I was crazy; my hair was falling out of the bun. I had it pinned; I didn't have time to put on any makeup since I was in a rush to get to the party. As I put my hair back in a messy bun, I heard someone playing the beginning of Brian McKnight's "One last cry." I opened the bathroom door and followed the sound of the piano down the hall to a door that was slightly adjarred. I picked my head in curiosity as to who was playing my favorite song so effortlessly. A man dressed in an all-white Armani suite sat at a black baby grand piano with his back towards the door. He began singing the first verse, "My shattered dreams and broken heart are mending on the shelf. I saw you holding hands standing close to someone else. Now I sit all alone, wishing all my feelings gone. I'd give my best to you nothing for me to do but have one last cry." His voice was deep and full; he sounded like a cross between Luther and Tank. I got so lost in him singing the chorus, 'One last cry, before I leave it all behind, I have got to put you out of my mind this time. Stop living a lie. I guess I'm down to one last cry." There was so much conviction in his voice; you would have believed that he had just expected losing the love of his life... Just as he was about to start the second verse, I lost my balance and fell face-first into the room. As I scrambled to get off the floor, he had moved across the room in three long strides to help me off the floor. When I looked up, ready to apologize for intruding, my words got caught in my throat as his grey eyes stared at me. I stared into his eyes; I felt a chill move down the small of my back; I felt like he was looking past my heart and straight into my soul. The moment his hand connected with mine to help me off the floor, I felt an immediate shock that he must have felt because he jumped back too. For a moment, the look of sexual desire and familiarity crossed his storming grey eyes but quickly replaced with confusion. "Are you okay? No one is supposed to be up here," he said with a smooth, silky deep voice. Still shook by the tingling sensation in between my legs; I was unable to speak. "Miss, are you okay?" He repeated, looking down at me. His 6'2 frame hovered over my 5'2 body. "I, I, I," I tried to say, with a shaky voice, never removing my eyes from his gaze. "I, I, I, yes, I am," I said as I leaned on the wall next to the door for support as I got up from the floor. "I am so sorry; I was going to use the bathroom, and I heard your piano and singing." I looked up at him only to see that his eyes were roaming the now exposed thigh. The black skirt I had on somehow ended up rolled up so high you could almost see my black lace boy shorts. "Did he just lick his lips?" I said to myself as I quickly tried to push my skirt back in place. No, I had to have just imagined that but the throbbing between my legs let me know that I was not. "Again, I am so sorry for interrupting," I said as I tried to walk back out the door. I was stopped by his quick motion to slam the door shut. I looked at him in panic and confusion but staring back at me was lust and desire. He walked towards me, causing me to back up into the wall next to the door. He was so close that I could feel the heat rising from his skin as he took his hand and brushed a piece of hair that had flown into my face. As he pushed the strand of hair behind my ear, his pointer finger traced the outline of my face. My breathing quickened with his every touch; as my lips parted to say something, he slides his finger to trace my lips. I don't know what compelled me to do what came next. I licked his finger with the tip of my tongue and looked directly into his eyes as I continued my pursuit and took his finger in and out of my mouth, sucking and licking as if his fingers were an ice cream cone. He released a deep moan from his lips, never breaking our stare down.

His hands slid down my back until he slowly lifted it, cupped my ass, and picked me up. As I wrapped my legs around his waist, I could feel the thickness of his dick press against my thigh. Just as his mouth took mine, I felt him unbuckle his pants, and he exposed that he was free balling, what a day for him to do that. His kisses tasted like peppermint and whiskey, a taste I could never be full of. He tore off the purple thong I had on, and as if it was the last pussy he was going to have, he entered me with urgency. I looked down at his erected penis and thought it had to the most smooth and gorgeous piece of dick I had ever seen. He had at least to be 10 inches with a slight left curve. A soft moan released from my lips as I felt him flicker his tongue over my nipples through my bra. He quickly releases my right breast, taking it into his mouth, sucking like he was a newborn baby. The electric feeling, I felt as he pushed his manhood inside my walls had my head spinning, ready to cum. He let out a loud ground as my pussy swallowed every inch, he was thrusting in. His strokes started off slow; he would push in and out. I shifted against the wall so that I could rock my hips to match his rhythm. With every stroke, I felt like he was going deeper, like he was leaving an imprint so that anyone who came after him would know he had been there. Just as I felt myself about to cum, I heard high heels walking up to the door and a voice calling out, "Durrell," "Durrell," and then came a knock on the door, "D, baby, are you in here?" Durrell snapped his head up from sucking on my neck but never removing himself from inside of me, he was still stroking me, another knock with a jiggle of the door, but it was locked. So that is his name, I thought as I tried to push Durrell from inside of me, he stood firm and held my arms above my head with one hand, and with the other, he put it to his lips and whispered, "shh, love." He smiled and kept stroking me, with the stroking rhythm mixed with the smooth, creamy sound of his voice, which had me ready to scream. When the knocking stopped and the sound of heels clicked back down the hallway, his thrusting became faster and harder. He cupped my face, which made me look directly into his eyes. I felt an orgasm creep up from my feet to my back; my head began spinning, making me feel like I was drunk. His eyes never left mine as both of us began to climax. Durrell let out a loud grunt and smacked my ass as he pumped in and out of me vigorously. I swear he was so deep I thought he was going to bust my guts open. Oh, shit, I thought to myself, as my head began to un-cloud itself. Just as Durrell pulled out of me, some of the leftover cum spilled from his head; I swear I wanted so bad to get on my knees and lick it all up, but the sound of the music playing downstairs startled me, and the reality of what just happened hit me. I started to panic and felt the need to run. Before he could even say two words to me, I unlocked the door and made a quick dash down the hall while trying to fix my skirt and shirt.

DURRELL

efore I could even fix my pants, the chocolate woman I had just fucked, ran out the door. "Hey, wait," I yelled down the hall after her. As I adjusted myself and took off down the hall to head downstairs, I was stopped by Nichole, my on and off again girlfriend walked out of my bedroom, which was right before the stairs. "D, there you are, I was looking for you, baby," she said as she walked up to me and pulled me into a forced hug. "Uhh hey, Nikki, (my nickname for her) I was uhh," I said, slipping out of her arms. "I was uhh, headed downstairs to the party," as I tried to get past her to go down the stairs to see where the beauty had gone. Nichole grabbed my hand and pulled me back towards my room, "That can wait, baby," she said, giving me her sexy smile, which usually would make my knees buckle, but the only thing on my mind was finding *her*. Knowing what Nikki wanted, I had to think of something quick before she smelled the still scent of the pussy I was just deep within. "Baby, why don't you go downstairs and grab us some drinks while I finish getting ready for the show," I said as I walked into my room and took my shirt off, placing it on my massive king-size bed. Nikki pouted and looked like she was about to throw a fit, but the moment she saw my rippled chest, she smiled and said, "Okay daddy, but tonight you are mine." I gave her a fake smile as she walked out the door. I walked over to the door and locked it, not trusting that

Nikki or any other person wouldn't try to sneak in while I was in the shower. I walked into my bathroom and stared at myself in the mirror, shaking my head and replaying what had just happened in the piano room.

TRACIE

eep, Beep. That is the sound I kept hearing as I slowly tried to open my eyes.

Beep, Beep, Beep. "Damn, that sound is annoying," I thought to myself. As I was trying to adjust my eyes to the bright light, I tried sitting up and noticed all the monitors around me started going off. That's when I saw my mom sitting to the right of me. "Tracie, don't move, honey, let me go get the doctor." Just as she was done saying it, a big manly looking nurse and the doctor walked in. I tried to speak and ask what the hell was going on and why I was in the hospital, but I felt a deep pain from the tube down my throat. Panic set in, and before I could rip the tube out my throat, the manly-looking nurse walked over and grab my hand, "Now, let's not make a fuss," she said as she injected some clear liquid into my IV. "No, No, No," I was trying to scream. "Please, I don't want to go back to sleep. I just want to know what happened." I just wanted to scream; my eyelids felt like a stack of bricks were being weighted on them; I saw HIM come into the room as I gave in to the darkness.

NICHOLE

He must think he is slick; I said to myself as I walked back down the stairs to the party and headed to the bar. "Shit, I need a drink." I was trying not to look too pissed off. "Whiskey please with no ice," I said to the bartender. "Right away, Miss Wright," he said. As he made my drink, I turned to survey the party. The room was filled with celebrities, models, and music executives, all here to celebrate Durrell's 30th birthday. "That Negro must think I am dumb if he thought that I didn't see that hood rat running down the stairs and him coming out of the music room. Which, by the way, he doesn't even let me go in smelling straight like pussy. I'll be damned if he thinks I am letting that shit slide. "Calm down, Nikki, keep it together," the voice inside my head told me. "Stick to the plan, just a few more months." "Miss, your drink," the bartender said, snapping me back into the room. "Oh, thank you very much," I said as I took the drink and headed towards the front of the room, where there was a medium-size stage set up for the band. I took the seat right next to the stage, so I could have a good view of the entire room, and most importantly, the stairs that I knew Durrell would come down any moment, and just like clockworks, down he walked. He was wearing a midnight blue tailored Armani suit, with a white shirt and matching Armani loafers. Damn, heard one of the girls saying as Durrell made his way through the sea of people, shaking his hand and wishing him happy birthday. "Shit, he looks good enough to eat." "I would let him hit it anytime he wants," two models from American's Top Model said next to me. I cleared my throat and said loud enough for them to hear, "Yea, too bad he won't be available cause he will be eating and hitting me all night." I didn't even wait to see the look of disgust and jealousy on their faces as I sashayed over to Durrell and looped my hand around his arm. "Baby, what took you so long?" I said loudly enough for anyone close to us to hear, "Everyone been waiting on you; what could have possibly taken the birthday boy away from his own party?" Looking at him with piercing eyes. Durrell squeezed my hand that was wrapped around his arm, and with a forced smile, he leaned in close and said, "Now dear, let's not make a scene; we will speak later," and gave me a slight kiss on my cheek, released my hand and walked to the side of the stage where the band was setting up. I couldn't believe he just dismissed me like that and in front of all these people. Who the fuck did he think I was? I started thinking as I made my way back to my seat. Did he just really dismiss me like that, and hell yeah, he better believe we are going to talk about this shit later. BRRT BRRT, my vibrating cell phone snapped me out of my trance. "You got to stop acting out," the voice in my head said. I took a deep breath and tried to calm down as I opened up the text message I just received. "SHE IS AWAKE" From :D ... I smiled hard AS the voice in my head said to me, "PERFECT."

MESHIA

What the hell is wrong with me? I asked myself as I ran out to the front door to my car. What am I thinking? I can't believe that I just fucked a random stranger. "I need to get it together," I said aloud, making it to my car. Then I realized, "Shit, my keys are in the kitchen, in that house." As I started walking back up to the back entrance of the house that leads to the kitchen, I could hear Renee screaming at my staff. As I entered the kitchen, Renee spotted me and said, "There you are, where have you been. I have been looking all over for you. I need you to finish the cakes, and the honoree is about to come down for a speech." "I just uh, I was." Renee looked at me with suspicion and gave me a look that said we would talk about this later. Relived that she wasn't going to make a scene in front of the staff, I began barking out orders while washing my hands and grabbing a new chef hat. Less than 20 minutes later, everything was ready to be served, and the red velvet double chocolate cake that I was known for was completed. As the party continued and the staff was moving the food in and out of the kitchen, I sat down at the kitchen table, completely exhausted and glad that this day was almost over. As I began changing out of my chef jacket, in walks Renee. "Oh no, don't take that off just yet. My client has requested you at the party to thank you personally. I looked at her rolling my eyes. "You are going to owe me big for this, just you wait," as she dragged me by my arm into the great front room. As soon as we entered the room, I could feel his gaze on me. I didn't know where he was in the room, but I could sense him, almost taste him. Get it together, Mesh. Just as we got to the front of the room, there HE was smiling until our eyes connected. I recognized the flicker of passion and longing in his eyes. Renee pushed me closer. "I would like to introduce the mastermind behind tonight's amazing meals and to the one and only Chef Meshia Young. The room exploded in applause and nods of approval. All except that chick who was nasty to me earlier. Durrell walked up beside me and took my hand in his and kissed it. "Chef Meshia Young huh," a playful look in his eye. "Nice to meet you again. Thank you for your amazing talent. I most enjoyed the sweet chocolate dessert you offered; I meant created." Renee stepped between, saying: "Meshia, this is Durrell, you know the Grammy winner and platinum singer... I hadn't realized that you all had met." "Durrell, baby, there you are," said the icy queen, giving me the once overlook. He was too busy licking his lips and smiling at me to notice that she had even said anything, let alone walked up. "D," she wined. Renee sensing the tension, said, "And of course, let me introduce you to Meshia, Nichole B Whittmen." The icy queen stepped in between Durrell and me and placed her hand around his waist, which snapped him out of the stare-down trance. He was probably undressing me again with his eyes, "Chef Meshia, is it, how do you do? I am Durrell's *Fiancé*," Nichole said in a stern voice, giving me a look that said, "Yeah bitch, this dick is mine." "Uhh Nikki, we are NOT Engaged," Durrell finally spoke up, "I told you about telling people that shit," he said, sounding annoyed. "Well, we are almost engaged baby, it's what I meant," Nichole said, turning her back to me, blocking Durrell's view of me. With all this shade this black plastic barbie was throwing me, and the heated longing look from Durrell and the WTF is going on look from Renee, I started to feel like I was going to pass out. "If you, please excuse me. I need some air," I said as I rushed out the front door that had been opened as more guests walked in. Rushing so fast from the house, I must not have seen the step that had just caused me to trip and to fall into someone coming up the walkway.

MARKUS

Man, Durrell is going to kill me for being late to his birthday album release party, being that I am his manager, I should have been at the party two hours ago, but with everything happening over the past couple of weeks, even sleeping and eating have had become a chore. With Tracie still in her coma and visiting the boys in the NCIU every day and night, I barely have had time to do anything. I pulled up to the front entrance of Durrell's house and could see the party was in full swing. As I got out of the car and handed the keys to the valet, I made myself a promise that tonight, I was going to let loose and enjoy the hard work I had helped throughout Durrell's career. I mean shit, I am the brains behind his success. I chuckled to myself, walking up to the front entrance. Suddenly, I felt something, or someone fall into me, forcing me to the ground. "Hey, what the hell," I said as a woman ran right into my chest. "You should watch," I stopped mid-sentence as the woman looked up into my eyes. "Mesh," I said quietly, feeling a little taken back and surprised to see her, HERE of all places.

MESHIA

I couldn't believe my damn luck. Out of ALL the people in the world I run into, it had to be him. "Mesh, What. How... What," Markus said as he tried to help me up from the ground. I snatched my arm away from him and turned to continue to my car, but before I could take another step, Markus stepped in front of me, blocking my way. "Meshia, I, look, well I," I covered my ears with my hands and said, "Save it, you jack ass, I don't have shit to say to you. By the way, how is Tracie?" Just before he had a chance to reply, the front door to the house opened up, and someone yelled, "Markus, there you are. We have been waiting for you." Markus turned to respond to the voice calling him, which allowed me the chance to move past him. I took off running and got into my car before he could turn back around and reach me. "Meshia," I heard him calling as I drove down the driveway, away from the sexy musician and my once baby daddy.

Once I was a few miles from the house, I pulled over so I could text Renee that I had left and Juan would finish the party, that I didn't feel good, and would call her in the morning. Just as I pressed send, tears began to fall. I just had the best sex of my life and saw Markus. It was just too much for one day. "Fuck Meshia," I said as I put the car into drive and headed home.

MARKUS

"I couldn't believe what I just saw, Meshia of all places here, and damn did she look good. From what I could tell, she wasn't pregnant anymore. What the hell was she doing here? Fuck, she looked good as hell, hips thick and her breast plumper than I remember," I said to myself as I walked toward the front of the mansion. Just as I stepped into the main room, I saw her. Ugh, my luck was horrible tonight, as I made eye contact with Nichole. She licked her lips and winked. I tilted my head and waved and asked the bartender, "Hennessy Straight." "Here you are, sir," the bartender said, handing me my drink. "Thanks," I said as I took a big sip and allowed the liquor to ease the tension that was developing in my neck ever since I saw Meshia. What is the chance that after three months, I would see her here of all places? I mean, I knew her catering business had gained some traction; she was an amazing cook. That's one of the reasons I fell for her in the first place. "Yo Markus, you finally decided to grace us with your presence," Durrell said, walking up. I could tell that he had already had a few drinks by the goofy grin he had on his face. "Yes, Mr. Markus, what has kept you from gracing us with your presence," she said, walking up behind Durrell, grabbing his waist, placing kisses on his neck. The hairs on my neck stood up at just the sound of her voice. I looked at her straight in her eyes before taking another sip of my drink. "Well, Hello Nichole, nice to see you're still creeping, I mean hanging around." Nichole cut me a look with her eyes that made me uncross my legs and fidget with my jacket. "Now, Markus, let's play," Nichole said. "Baby, why don't you go ahead and start your set, and Markus and I will go check on what's keeping your cake?" She gently turned Durrell in the direction of the stage at the front of the room. "I will Holla at you later Mack Man," using his nickname for me, which I fucking hated, Durrell said, swaying a little as he walked away. Nichole stepped closer to me. I could smell her Juicy Couture Viva La Juicy Perfume. She had been wearing that since the day I met her. Nichole bit her lower lip and pouted; she sashayed away towards one of the bathrooms down the hallway from the party. "Fuck it," I said as I downed the rest of my drink and followed my wife's best friend down the hall.

NICHOLE

I knew his thirsty ass was going to follow me. If there is anything I know about Markus La'Mont Damon, it is that he can't resist pussy and money. I made my way into the bathroom and waited for him to come in, and sure enough, in comes Markus. "I thought I told you to stay away from my clients," he said as he walked closer to me, making my back hit the porcelain vanity. "Now, you know I have never been too good with directions, and what difference is it to you, jealous that Durrell is hitting this pussy right every night," I said, knowing this was going to make him mad. Markus's face twisted up in anger but slowly turned into a naughty grin. "Oh really, Nik, I bet he doesn't make you cream like I do with just one stroke," he said as he picked me up and sat me on the vanity. "I bet he doesn't lick your walls better than I do." I tried to find the words for a comeback, but all I could do was focus on the throbbing and heat from between my legs. "Why don't you remind me," I said as I slid my legs further open to allow him to see that I was not wearing any panties. "Fuck," he said as he dropped to his knees and slipped his tongue up and down my clit. I pushed his head further into my pussy, "Hmm, yes, like that," I said.

He licked and sucked and twisted his tongue, "Flip that shit," the voice in my head said. "This isn't a part of the plan." "Shut up, this feels good," I said to the voice, for once finally being able to stand up to her. As I focused on the euphoria I was feeling from Markus's tongue, I tuned out the other voices that were yelling in my head. I heard Durrell on stage singing his single, "For the Love of it All."

TRACIE

EEP BEEP. That's all I heard as I slowly opened my eyes. BEEP BEEP. "Damn, why does that machine have to be so damn loud," I thought to myself as I tried to lift my head to see what was causing all that damn noise. It took me a minute to adjust my eyes to the bright ass lights; I started to panic as I realized that I was in a hospital bed and that I couldn't move. I tried again to turn my head and raise my hand up, but nothing, wtf, nothing. I tried again and again, and nothing. Suddenly, all the monitors in my room began to go off with a louder alarm, and in rushed a nurse who looked to be in her 50s and a tall black doctor. "Tracie, can you hear me," the doctor said as he rushed to my bed, flashing a bright light into my eyes, going from pupil to pupil. "Tracie, my name is Dr. Kenneth Dwayne James Bryant. I need you to calm down. Try to take deep breaths," he said as the nurse adjusted the monitors. I tried to speak, but my throat was so sore and felt like cotton was stuffed down it. "MMM mmm," I said as tears rolled down my eyes. "Tracie, it's okay, take your time. We had to place a tube down your throat to help you breathe; just relax and keep breathing." "Should we sedate her again?" The nurse asked the doctor like I wasn't even in the room. He shook his head, "No," and never taking his eyes off me. "Tracie, I need you to listen to me; you have been in a medically induced coma for three months. It will hurt a little for you to speak right away. If you can, blink twice for me if you understand. Okay, good. This is Nurse Troy, she is going to help assist me with getting you back to normal, but right now, we are going to give you some medicine to help get your levels back down." "No, No, No, I am tired of sleeping, please," I said in my head, tears rolling down my face. Dammit, why can't I get the words out ... Come on, T, you can do this .. NNNNO, I finally heard my voice say. The doctor and the nurse looked at me with shock. "No," I this time whispered louder, coughing as the air hit my lungs. "I am tired of being in the dark."

MARKUS

I know what you all are thinking, WTF, Shit I was thinking the same thing as I followed Nichole to that bathroom, but it had been a few months since I had her. I knew it was wrong, especially with her being my wife's best friend and the fact she was lying up in the hospital in a coma. But there's something about Nichole that I can't seem to get out of my system. I mean, I had been fucking her since she was an intern at my record label. She was the perfect piece of ass, even after I met and married Tracie. She became friends with Tracie and was around all the damn time, trying to fuck me every chance she had. But it wasn't until she started that bull shit talk about me leaving Tracie for her. Please, I would never wife such a whore and gold digger as her. At first, I was pissed when she started dating Durrell, but then I was relieved cause Nichole seemed to be so focused on him than me, so for that, I was thankful. Brtt, Brtt, Brtt, the sound of my phone going on off in my pocket brought me back to the now. I pulled my head from between Nichole and reached for my phone. "NOOOOOOO, don't stop, baby," Nichole said, whining because she was so close to nutting. She tried to reach out for me, but I stepped back and pulled my phone out. "Hello, this is M." "Hello, this is Dr. Bryant from Baylor and White. I wanted to let you know that your wife is awake." My mind went completely crazy, and my phone dropped to the floor. I started to feel the Henny creeping back up on me. Nichole got down from the vanity and began to clean herself off. "Are you okay?" "Hello, Hello sir, are you there?" I picked up the phone, trying to get my words together, "Uhh, yes Doc, I am. Uhh, is she talking? Is she asking for me?" "Yes, she is talking but only a few words; she was a little startled when she first woke up. We gave her a sedative to calm her down. She should be back awake any moment again." "Uhh, thank you, Doctor. I will be there right away," I said as I sat on the toilet. I hung up my phone and held it in my hands, trying to take in what the Doctor just told me. "Markus, what's wrong?" Nichole said as she looked at me via the reflection of the mirror. I just stared back at her, "Tracie is awake."

TRACIE

eep, Beep. That was the first sound I heard when I woke the second time. I slowly opened my eyes, slightly blinded by the brightness of the lights in the room. My head was throbbing and hurting, and I was thirsty as hell. After my eyes adjusted to the light, I looked around to see that it wasn't just a nightmare; I was in a hospital room. Just as I tried to sit myself up, a handsome man in a white coat and an elderly woman following him walked into the room. The nurse rushed over to quiet the monitors as she pushed up my bed so that I could sit upright. "Tracie, do you remember where you are or how you got here." "I am in the hospital," I said with a crack in my voice. I cleared my thought, "And I don't remember how I got here, what happened to my babies." Dr. Bryant walked over to my bed and grabbed my hand. "Your boys are fine; they are in the NICU because they were underweighted and had a problem breathing on their own. Once we check you out, we can have the nursing staff take you to see them." I was trying to process what he was saying, but all I could focus on was his handsome face and gentle brown eyes. His butterscotch skin tone was so smooth, and his goatee was edged up with perfection. When he took his thick tongue and ran it slowly over his full lips, slowly wetting them, I thought I was going to cream right there in front of him and the nurse. "Tracie, Tracie, "Dr. Bryant said, snapping my attention back. "Oh yes, I heard you, my babies,"

I said, shifting in the bed, starting to feel uncomfortable under his gaze, and the fact that I could even be thinking about how good it would feel to have his tongue licking on my clit. "Are you sure you're okay," Dr. Bryant said, releasing my hand, sensing my discomfort. "We can give you something to make you comfortable." "NO," I shouted a little too loudly. "I am okay." "Okay, great," Dr. Bryant said, giving me a smile that took my breath away. "I will let Nurse Troy finish things up. I will be back later to check on you. If you need me, just have the staff page me, and I will give your parents and husband a call to let them know you're awake. My husband, thinking about Markus for the first time since I woke up, shit yes, I was married, and yet all I could think about was watching that tone and seemed firm ass attached to Dr. Bryant walk out the door. What the fuck is wrong with me? Here I am married, with newborn twins, just woke up from a fucking coma, a fucking coma; how the fuck did I end up in that bitch in the first place? And where the fuck is Markus in the first place? Why the fuck isn't he here? I thought to myself as I let the nurse finish her tests.

DURRELL

My head was spinning. Shit so was the room. I had way too much to drink. As I made my way up my stairs headed to my bedroom, the party had ended about 30 minutes ago. Some of my boys were passed out in the living room, and some in the spare rooms. Whenever I threw a party, I always had Uber rides for the guests who were too drunk to drive and let my close friends crash in any of the five spare rooms I had. I knew I was drunk when I hit the top of the stairs, and instead of heading to my bedroom, I went into the music room, my memories of fucking Chef Meshia before the party and how she just rushed out. I knew by the look in her eyes when Renee introduced us that she was surprised and had no clue who I really was. And I also remember the look she had given me when Nichole walked up and introduced herself as my fiancée. She looked pissed as hell. My dick started to get hard as I remembered how she tasted, how natural it felt to have her in my arms, how tight and hot her pussy felt as I slipped my dick in. Shit, that was the craziest and erotic thing I have ever done with a stranger, and raw at that, but damn, it felt so right. I smiled and stumbled back down the hallway. I passed a few of the spare rooms and heard moans and groans of pleasure. Shit, someone was getting their back blown out with all that moaning. As I entered my room, I stumbled out my loafers and didn't even bother undressing anything else. I sprawled out over my King size bed face up, trying to think how I was going to get in touch with Meshia again. My mind started drifting back to earlier in the music room, her moans and how hard she made me with just her scent. I must have been really drunk cause I swore I felt her hands unbuckling my pants and freeing my dick from my pants and taking it into her mouth. I tried to raise my head up to look down at her, but her mouth on my dick, and my buzz was feeling too good. "Oh shit, baby," I grabbed a hand full of her hair and pushed her head down further on my dick, "Oh yea, just like that, baby." She moved her mouth up and down my shaft while taking me deep into her throat. I lost it when she grabbed my ball sack with both hands. "Shit, I am about to cum," I bellowed out and thrust in and out of her mouth faster. "Shit," I said as my body released my cum into her mouth. "Damn Meshia," I said as I released my load. "Fuck," I pumped in and out of her mouth until every last drop was out of my balls. I collapsed back onto my bed and passed out, thinking, "Shit, that was one hell of a dream."

NICHOLE

Did he really just scream out that bitch's name while I was the one with his dick in my mouth, making him feel this good, like a fuckin slap in the face, I thought to myself, as I got up from the floor, careful not to trip, grabbed my purse, and a pillow and headed to the bathroom. I only had a small window of time to get this done. I closed the bathroom door with my hand and turned on the light, careful not to drop the condom I had just rolled off Durrell. I looked at myself in the mirror, the person looking back at me I didn't even recognize. I started to have doubts about what I was about to do, and the voice in my head said, "You deserve this; make them pay." I pulled out the plastic container marked "Sperm" and emptied the condom full of cum into the container, making sure not to spill any of it onto the counter. "This shit better work," I said as I pulled out a plastic syringe and placed it into the container, sucking up all the sperm into it. My phone lit up with a text message from "Doc." "Did you do it yet?" I sent a reply, "Not yet, about to inject now." "Ok. Make sure to lay on your back with your feet in the air for at least 30 minutes." "I know, I know. You don't have to remind me. I will text you once I am done."

I laid my phone back on the counter, pulled my dress up and took the syringe, and laid on the carpeted floor with the pillow under my butt. "It's now or never," I said to the voice in my head. I spread my legs, took a deep breath, and inserted the syringe as deep as it would go into my vagina as possible, and released the sperm. I laid the empty syringe next to me, and I lifted my legs up in the air. "This shit better work, after all the work I had put into this plan."

After sitting on the floor with my legs lifted for 30 minutes, I got up and put the syringe and the container back into my purse. I took a hot wash, clothed, and cleaned between my legs. I wrapped the condom in a tissue and stuck it in the trash and washed my hands. Before I left the bathroom, I took out my phone and sent back a text, "It's done, this better work." Brt, Brt, "Trust me, it will" was the reply. I turned my phone off, stuck it back into my purse, and walked back into the bedroom to see that Durrell had gotten undressed and was sleeping naked on top of the sheets. I looked at his gorgeous fit body, appreciating that he went to the gym three times a day, no days off. Too bad he had to go and fuck everything up and sleep with that trick. I went to the dresser and grabbed one of his t-shirts and changed into it. I tried to push Durrell over so that I could pull the covers up over him as I got into the bed, but he was dead weight, so I pulled the covers over myself and laid in the bed. I need this plan to work out. I was so close to getting everything I wanted. "Meshia," Durrell mumbled as he rolled over. I wanted to smack his ass upside his head, but the voice said, "Just think nine months." I smiled, hoping and praying that I did get pregnant.

DURRELL

amn, my head is pounding, I thought to myself as I rolled over, but shit, that was one hell of a dream I had last night about Meshia. It felt so real and felt so good. I definitively had too much to drink. As my eyes adjusted and I turned over to get out of my bed, I couldn't move because there was an arm draped across me. I looked over and saw someone that was in bed with me. Maybe it wasn't a dream, but how did Meshia end up coming back. I was excited as I pulled the cover off to expose the face, but I was quickly disappointed when I saw Nichole's face and not Meshia. What the hell happened last night? How did she end up in my bed? I felt myself getting ready to be sick, so I moved her arm quickly and headed to the bathroom to throw up. I heard Nichole turn over and say, "Baby, are you okay?" Just the sound of her voice made me puke harder. I finished throwing up, rinsed my mouth out, brushed my teeth, and head back into my room. Nichole was sitting on the bed, comfortable with the covers barely covering her chest. "You feel better now," she asked. "Uhh, yea. Thanks. I guess I had way too much to drink last night," I said, walking over to my nightstand and pulled out a bottle of aspirin. I swallowed it down without any water. I sat back down on the bed, and Nichole came up and wrapped her arms around my neck. "So, what are our plans today? Shopping and lunch." "Uhh yeah, about that, Nikki," I said, turning around to face her and removing her arms from me. "I don't think so, I uhh; I think we need to take a break. That stunt you pulled last night introducing yourself as my fiancée was too much. I keep telling you we aren't ready for that, not at this point in my career." Nichole pouted, and for a quick second, I could have sworn I saw a crazed look in her eyes. "Durrell, seriously, you are upset about that. Come on now. Why shouldn't I introduce myself as your fiancée? We have been together forever anyway, and your publicist already said it would boost your album sales if you were to get married, so now you trying to break up with me?" "What?" Tears started to form in her eyes. "Nikki, don't start crying. I do appreciate you, but I see now that we are in two different places; I just need some time to myself to focus on my music," I said, trying not to look at her in the face because I knew if I did, she would see that I was lying through my teeth. I mean, I wasn't completely lying; I did need to focus on my music more, but it would be much easier to get Meshia back in my bed without Nichole around. It was just something about the instant connection and feeling that Meshia gave me; I had to find out why that was. "Look, Nikki," "Uhh no, you look, Durrell," Nichole interrupted me loudly. "You think I am dumb, huh? You think I don't know that this is about that chick from yesterday. You are going to try and tell me you all of a sudden need a break. Please, I saw the way you were looking at her. It was distasteful and weak as hell. What you're not going to do is sit here and lie to me and say it was about me saying I was your fiancée. That's not the first time I have done that; now it's an issue because it was in front of that hood rat chef. Her fucking food wasn't even that great. I saw her come out of the music room last night. I heard what was happening in there with you and her, and you have some fucking nerve to say you need a fucking break." I just stood there looking shocked as fuck. I was trying to think of something to say, but shit, how the fuck did she know. "I don't think the media would like to know that little miss chef is out here hoeing with your ass in a music room; we wouldn't want that to get out now, would we, Durrell?" Nichole said as she put her clothes on and fluffed her hair. "Nichole, look, about that, I, it just happened, but this has nothing to do with what happened with Meshia. This is about you and me, and I know you're not going to the media cause then you would look bad too, so stop with the dramatic shit and get the fuck up out my house." I walked back over to my bed and laid down. "Oh really, Durrell? You think I won't go to the media, uhh? This shit is far from over. Mark my words, that bitch is going to bring nothing but drama, and no boo, you and I are far from being over. I'll leave right now, but you better believe that you and I are far from being over. WE will never be over," she said as she grabbed her purse and slammed my bedroom door. "Fuck," I said. How the fuck did I put up with her crazy ass for so long. But there was something about the way Nichole said, "We are far from over." I believed her.

MESHIA

I still couldn't believe what I was looking at as I stepped into my office at my restaurant in uptown Dallas. I had just opened it up a few weeks, and we already had reservations booked every night till the end of the year. My assistant Shanice walked in from the kitchen. "Hey boss lady, someone has an admirer," she said, looking at the tulip bouquets that filled my office. "When did all this arrive," she said, moving around to my desk, smelling the pink color bouquet. "This morning. The delivery guy showed up right after I opened the doors." "You didn't tell me that you were dating anyone," Shanice said as she handed me the menu for this evening's dinner crowd. "That's cause I am not," I said. "Is there a card or note from who they are from?" Shanice asked, looking around one of the vases. I looked at the vase on my desk, which was the biggest of the arrangements, and noticed an envelope attached to it. I picked it up, and Shanice said, "OHH, what does it say? What does it say?" "Uhh, don't you need to get going on the prep for this evening?" I looked at Shanice as I played with the envelope, sitting down in my desk chair. Shanice looked at me with a grin, "Alright, boss lady, but whoever this mystery person is, he sure knows how to make a statement," she looked at all the vases. I smiled at her. Shanice was a hard-working single mother of two wonderful kids. "Why don't you stop by after this evening's shift and take as many vases home as you want? Lord knows I can't fit all these in my condo." "Really? Oh, that would be so nice. Thank you, boss lady," she said with a big grin on her face as she walked to the door. "Oh, I should mention for tonight, someone booked the entire restaurant with a full menu, and they made a special request for you to make an appearance before the meal course is presented." "Oh, really? Okay, well, that's wonderful. Do we know who it was; ballplayer, actor, politician?" I asked, still playing with the envelope in my hands. "Uhh no, the assistant that called in said the guest wanted to remain anonymous for extra privacy. I assume it's a popular actor or a player from the Cowboys," Shanice said. "Hmm, that's interesting. Okay, thank you for the update. Let's get everyone together for a rundown of the menu. We need everything perfect, as this could be a great opportunity for us to get exclusive clientele." "Will do, boss lady," Shanice said as she closed my office door. "Interesting," I said aloud to myself. "Well, let's see who all this is from." Markus was the first person to pop into my head since I had seen him a few days earlier. He was the only person besides Renee who knew what my favorite flower was. My stomach started to churn, and I had butterflies as I opened the envelope. "Not even these gorgeous flowers can compare to the beauty that God has blessed you with," read the note. I turned the note over to see if who sent it had written their name on the back, but nothing. I reread the note again. This was too nice to come from Markus; he would have just written something simple like "I want to fuck again" or some dumb shit like that. I put the card inside my desk drawer and leaned back in my chair, thinking who would have this much interest in me, maybe a client? They went over and beyond with the Thank you gift but nothing over the top like this. I stood up and smelled the bouquet that was sitting on my desk, and then it dawned on me. "No way," I said aloud. "But how did he? Would he? Why would he?" My clit started throbbing at the thought of Durrell. "How did he know my fav.," stopped mid-sentence and said, "Renee, I am going to kill her," and then pulling out my iPhone. I texted Renee, "I am going to kill you; why did you give him my info?" I pressed send, waiting on the immediate reply I knew that would come back. Brt, Brt, "Because that's what best friends are for," Renee replied. "Remind me to hit you next time I see you," I sent a text back. KNOCK KNOCK. I was so startled by the knock that I dropped my phone on the floor. "Yes, who is it?" "It's me, boss lady; everyone is waiting on you to start the meeting," Shanice said from the other side of the door. "Oh, okay, I'll be there shortly, thank you," I said as I pressed my legs together tightly to stop the throbbing. Get it together, Mesh; he is just a man. "Yeah, a really sexy and irresistible man," I said quietly. Once I got the throbbing to subside, I got up from the chair, fixed my skirt and pulled on my chef jacket and hat, and opened up my door to head to the meeting with my staff. Cooking would take my mind off Durrell and the fact I wasn't just some random fuck to him.

By the time my staff and I finished the prep work for this evening's secret guest's party, I had forgotten all about the flowers and Durrell. As I walked back into my office, my cell phone started ringing. "Go, best friend, that's my best friend, you betta you." "Hey Nene, (my nickname for Renee)." "Girl, now I know you been dodging my calls, so bitch, you better explain," Renee yelled into the phone. I sighed, "You know me too well. I am still trying to wrap my head around what happened, girl." I sat down in my office chair, slipping off my shoes. "I mean, one minute I was looking for the bathroom, to listening in on him playing the piano, to having the best sex I ever had, to his girlfriend almost walking in on us, to running out and bumping into Markus, to leaving. Shit, that was one hell of a fucking night." "WOW, that was one hell of a night, so the best sex you ever had, huh? Was it as big as they say it is? Is it round and thick? Does it have a curve? What was his stroke like? Oh shit, his girl almost walked in. Shit, shit," Renee said in one breath with excitement and questioning. "Slow down," I said, laughing. "I will say it is bigger than the blogs can imagine, and I am still trying to get the tingle to go away from between my legs." "Damn girl, really? ... well, I guess you won't mind that I ...."

"I won't mind that you did what?" My phone beeped, notifying me that my phone battery was about to die. "That I gave...." Click, my phone went dead. I rushed and opened my desk drawer looking for my extra phone charger, when Shanice came into my office. "Hey Meshia, there is a driver out front asking for you." "Okay, okay, give me a few. Have you seen my phone charger," I looked at her suspiciously? "Uh yeah, I took it home by mistake," Shanice said, not making eye contact. "How many times have I told you about not bringing my things back Shanice," I said, annoyed because now I wouldn't know what Renee meant til later when I got home to charge my phone. "I am sorry, I will bring it back tomorrow, but what do you want me to tell the driver?" Shanice asked, looking uncomfortable. "Oh yeah, uhh, I will go see what this is about."

I walked out to the front of my restaurant and saw a middle-aged black guy dressed in an all-black suit. "Are you, Ms. Young?" He asked as I approach. "Yes, I am. How can I help you?"

He handed me a white envelope with my name on it in the same font as the card from the flowers in my office. I looked at the driver questioning, "Please open the card once we are in the limo." "Limo," I said, looking out the window to see a black stretch limo parked out front. Shanice walked out from the back with several of my staff. "Who sent you?" I asked the driver. "I have been instructed to drive you to your appointment with or without force. I raised my eyebrows at him and gave him a look. "Well, I am not going anywhere till you tell me who sent you." I crossed my arms across my chest just as the door to the restaurant chimed.

Before I looked up at who had entered the door, the hairs on my arms started to tickle, and I felt butterflies in my stomach. My body reaction to the person who entered was confirmed when my staff started to "OH, OH, UHH, WOW. Is that? No, it can't be. Damn, he is even finer in person."

I looked up, surprised and knowing it was Durrell, looking like he just stepped out of a GQ magazine cover. "Well, you are one hard lady to surprise," he said, walking up beside the driver. "Thank you, Mike. I will take it from here." "Yes, sir," Mike, the driver, said and walked out the door. I was frozen in my position and tried to find some words to say to this God-like man standing in front of me. "Why didn't you tell us you know the General?" Shanice and all my staff said as they began to circle around Durrell, asking him for his autograph and taking pictures of him. I was still stuck in a trance as I watched him smoothly handle my staff, especially the ladies. I could feel the heat coming from my lady as he smiled at me. Finally, I was able to find my voice. "Okay, guys enough, I am sure Mr. Babb's didn't come here to be swarmed and bothered; I don't pay you all to harass our guest," everyone sighed and thanked Durrell and reluctantly left the dining area back to the kitchen. Once everyone left, we were left alone. I looked at Durrell in his lustful grey eyes, "So Mr. Babb's, how did you find me, and most importantly to what do I owe the pleasure of this visit and flowers?"

DURRELL

I was nervous as hell, with Meshia looking me dead in my eyes. I didn't realize how deep brown they were. I felt like she was looking straight through directly to my soul. She looked away as I stared back, which gave me a chance to gain my focus. "The how I found you isn't important, and we both know you know the why," I said, taking a step in her direction, which caused her to back up into one of the chairs behind her. "I have no clue why Mr. Babbs?" Meshia said as she tried to move the chair in-between us. "Oh, you don't," I said as I pushed the chair out the way and grabbed her arm before she could move away again. "Well, why don't I remind you." I pulled her against my chest and cupped the back of her head and pushed my lips down onto hers. She tried to push away but gave in to the kiss. I wanted to savor every taste of her, wanted to take her right there in the middle of the restaurant, but we were interrupted by one of the waitresses. "Uhh, Chef, Juan needs you in the kitchen." As I looked into her eyes, I took my time letting go of her, her eyes moving from me to the young lady entering the room. Meshia tried to push out of my arms, but I held firm and turned to the young lady. "Tell Juan that Chef Young will be unavailable for the evening." The young lady looked confused, looking at Meshia. "Shanice, tell him I'll be right there," Meshia said as she pushed again to get out of my grasp. This time, I let her go, "And as for you, how dare you tell my staff what to do." The young lady stood frozen watching Meshia, and I go back and forth. "You have no right," Meshia kept saying, walking towards the kitchen door but stopping when I said, "Yes, I do. I am the client who booked your restaurant out for the night, and your motto is "do as the client says," at least that's what your website says." Meshia turned back towards me with a heated glaze, "You are the client, what? Why?" I cleared my throat. "Get in the car, and I will answer all your questions," I said, walking towards the door to the restaurant. "Durrell, seriously, I have my whole staff here cooking, and it is all for your games," Meshia said, sounding annoyed. "And the meals they are preparing are for a reason now, Chef Young. The car is waiting, and we are late," I said, holding open the door. "Shanice, tell Chef Juan to continue the preparation as the order ran, and I will be back soon. Call me on my cell if you need anything." "Yes, chef," Shanice said, smiling at me as she walked back to the kitchen. "Shall we?" I said to Meshia as she walked out the door and rolled her eyes at me. "This better be good, Durrell." "Oh, believe me, it is," I said, laughing as we got into the limo.

MARKUS

"Okay, get it together," I said to myself as I prepared myself to walk into Tracie's hospital room, hoping that she didn't remember the shit that happened that night. As I walked into her room, Tracie was laughing at something her Doctor, who was sitting on the edge of her bed rather too close for my liking, was telling her. I cleared my throat to let them know I was in the room, which neither one of them seemed to acknowledge my presence. "Well, Tracie, I will be back to check in on you later this evening," her Doctor said to her, shaking her hand a little too long. "Thank you, Dr. B; I appreciate ALL that you have done for me," Tracie said, smiling, a smile I hadn't seen come my way in months, even before that night. I cleared my throat again and walked over to Tracie's side. "Yes, thank you. Uhh, Doctor B is it, for all your professorial help," extending my hand out to remove Tracie from his. He looked up at me and said, "The pleasure has been all mine, Markus," as he turned to walk out the room, and before walking completely out of the room, I could have sworn I saw him smirking. "So, what the fuck was that all about," I said, turning to Tracie as I took the chair next to her bed. "Excuse me," she said with a look of disgust on her face. " I have been awake for more than 24 hours now, and your ass was nowhere to be found, and you come strolling in here asking questions. Uhh No, how about you start with why the fuck

I ended up here in this fucking hospital bed in the first place and where the fuck my babies are?" I could feel the tension in my neck starting to build up as I looked at my wife sitting in her hospital bed, looking mad and hurt, and I felt like shit because I was the reason, she was there in the first place. I grabbed her hand and said, "Your right baby, I am so sorry I wasn't here when you woke up. The babies are at home with Patrice. I can arrange for her to bring them here later if you want, and there is no excuse for me not to have been here right away; please forgive me. I am just glad you are finally awake, and I have my beautiful wife back." I gave her my you know I am sorry look and kissed the back of her hand, knowing that she has never been able to resist my smile and a hand kiss.

"Markus," she said, "I am glad to be awake too, and yes, please schedule for Patrice to bring the boys here to see me. I can't believe I have missed so much time with them already. I can't even believe that this happened to me." "I know, baby, I can't either," I said. "What happened that night? I can't remember anything from that night," she said, looking up at me as I caressed her hand in mine. "The doctors said you had a ruptured placenta, which caused you to go into labor early and pass out. I came out of the shower that night and found you on the floor," I said. It was at least part of the truth. "Hmm, really? I wonder what I was doing before that. The nurse said that my phone wasn't in my things. Do you, have it?" "I can have Patrice bring it over when she brings the boys over later today, sweetie." "Okay, baby. I just can't wait to get out of this hospital bed and back home with you and our boys, she said with tears in her eyes." "Don't cry, baby," I said as I kissed her forehead and cheeks. "You will be home soon. Why don't you try and get some rest before you meet our sons?" "Okay, baby," she said. "That's a good idea." I kissed her one last time on the cheek and said, "I love you, T." "I love you too," she said as I walked out the door. Once I was outside, I pulled out my phone, "Hey, meet me at the condo, and don't wear any panties?"

This nigga thinks I am dumb. He is probably about to go fuck God knows what. I bet it isn't the bitch he was planning to leave me for. Whoever that bitch is, Markus had another thing coming. He is the reason I am in this fucking hospital in the first place, why I missed out on so much time of my little babies' lives already. I am going to make Markus pay. My taste for revenge is strong, and the plan I thought of would hit him where it most mattered to him; his music, pockets, and his dick. He thought he was so smart by getting me to sign that prenup. "Oh, baby, just sign it. I am never going to leave you, nor you leave me, so it's like it won't even matter." That night, I actually believed him, but my momma is the lawyer who processed the paperwork, and she and my father never trusted Markus and so added in a little adultery clause that Markus didn't even bother to re-look at the prenup once I signed it. The clause states that if Markus commits proven adultery, I get 100 percent control of all his shares in the label, 95 percent of all assets and properties he owns, and full custody of any children we have at the time, and he pays 10,000 per child in child support. Thanks to my mom being an attorney and never trusting Markus from day one, she made sure to add that clause in after we signed it. It pays to have a mother who looks out for you. Now I just must figure out how I was going to catch his ass and put my plan in motion. First, I need to get my ass out this hospital and home with my babies.

NICHOLE

Just as I finished licking the last bit of cum drops from Markus's dick, his phone rang. He pushed my face from between his legs so that he could grab the phone from his pants pocket, which was on the floor. "Damn, Markus," I said as I caught myself before I fell to the floor. "Hush up," he said as he hit the screen to answer. "Hello, yes, baby. Sorry, I was in the studio and didn't hear my phone. Yes, T, I know what time it is," I rolled my eyes as I got off the floor to head to the bathroom so that I could clean up. Markus was too busy trying to pull up his pants, almost tripping over the ottoman that was in front of him. As I entered the bathroom, I heard Tracie on the other end of the phone yelling at the top of her lungs, "Get your ass here now." I closed the door and began laughing at the thought of just having sucked the life out of Markus and being the reason, he was late for whatever Tracie was screaming about. As I turned on the water and grabbed a washcloth to wash the excess cum that had dripped on my face, I looked in the mirror, and my reflection smiled back at me and said, "That nigga is no good. He just fucked the shit out your face but damn near breaking his neck at just a phone call from her, but you will have the last laugh on both of them." "Yea, you're right," I said to her. "I will miss that dick, though." Just then, the tracker app notification on my phone signaled. I dried my face and hands and picked up my phone from the countertop and tapped the app to see it say that Durrell's vehicle had left his house. I smiled, thinking adding that tracker to the bottom of his car was the smartest plan I had come up with. I needed to protect my investment and needed to know where that nigga was at all times in order for my plan to work. I wondered where he was going, so I pulled up a calendar app that allowed me to access his calendar (as I said, I need to protect my investment). "Mayor's Ball," 7:30 pm. Shit, how could I have forgotten that? Shit, we were supposed to go together. Well, that was before the argument we had. "Hmm, tonight will be the perfect time to make up. Durrell would make a scene in front of the camera," I said to her, staring back at me in the mirror. "Well, bitch hurry up and shower and get that ass to the ball," she said back to me as I turned on the shower. "Yep, tonight would be perfect for our reunion."

MARKUS

Once again, I was late, and Tracie was mad as hell at me when I arrived at the hospital 3 hours late. Damn, fucking around with Nikki had me late. The nanny had brought the boys to the hospital for Tracie to see them for the first time since she had come out of the coma. When I did arrive, she would barely even talk to me or look at me. She looked so beautiful holding both of our boys, it almost made me regret the fact that I was getting the life sucked out of me by Nikki, but damn, Nicki's head is too good to ever turn down. Shit, by the time I walked out of the hospital, Tracie wouldn't even look at me. She just kept cutting her eyes at me as I excused myself, saying I couldn't be late for the Mayor's ball that was happening tonight. Luckily, my parents and Tracie's parents were there to keep Tracie and the babies busy. "We are here, sir," my driver said as the car pulled up to the front of the downtown hall, where the ball was being held. I took a deep breath and finished my drink, shaking off my thoughts about Tracie and the boys. Tonight, was about business; I need to make sure that the mayor was going to sign off on the new studio site that I was trying to get built. I stepped out of the car, with flashing lights from photographers shouting, "This way, Markus, this way," as I walked down the make-shift red carpet, stopping only a few times before I made my way to the front door of the mansion. Before I stepped through the door, I heard someone shout, "Durrell, this way. Who is the lovely lady with you?" I turned expecting to see Nichole and Durrell, but who I saw made my heart drop out of shock. There standing close to Durrell was Meshia, in a red and black Gucci dress that showed way too much of the breast I used to hold and caress in my mouth. "What the fuck is she doing here with him?" I said to myself as I started to take a step towards Meshia, but a flash of the camera reminded me of where I was and that making a scene was not the best choice. Instead, I turned around and walked into the mansion, looking for the closest bar for a strong drink. Double shot of crown, no ice. I took the glass from the bartender and jugged it down. Just as I was about to tell the bartender to make it another, I felt her hand on my arm, making my dick jump to attention. There was only one person who could command my dick this way, fucking Nikki. "Hey, baby," Nikki said, cooing into my ear. I pulled my arm back and tried to shift my weight to hide what her touch had done to me. "UHH, Nikki, I am surprised to see you here. Uhh, what are you doing here," I said, trying to put a little distance between us? Nikki looked down at the bulge in my pants and smiled, "Why wouldn't I be here? My Man is here, so of course, I would be here." I looked at her, almost ready to laugh because she must not have gotten the memo that her "man" had moved on with my Meshia. That thought alone made my dick shrink back up. "I guess your man didn't know he was supposed to come with you," I said, as I motioned to the bartender, "Another double, please." Nikki looked at me with daggers in her eyes. "What is that supposed to mean, Markus. I don't have time for bullshit tonight." "Look, this isn't my business, so why don't you go find your man and see what is up with him," I said, taking a sip from my drink. "I will do just that,"

Nikki said, looking around the room, "I just have to find him first." I chuckled as she walked away. "Good luck with that."

DURRELL

"Y"ou look amazing," I said to Meshia as I led her through the crowd of other celebrities and photographers. They all seemed to part out of the way like I was Moses at the red sea. Meshia smiling shyly at me: "Thank you, you have amazing taste in fashion. This dress is amazing. I am not sure though how you knew my size." "Lol, I have my ways," I said, placing my hand on the small of her back and pulling her closer as we reached the dance floor in the front of the room.

The band began to play Brian McKnight's "One last cry" right on cue. "I believe this is our song. May I have this dance?" "Our song," she said, raising one eyebrow as she placed her head on my shoulder as we swayed slowly to the rhythm of the song. "Yes, our song," I said, as I began to quietly sing the words in her ear." There was a tap on my shoulder halfway through the song. "Who the fuck is this, Durrell?" Without evening having to turn around, I knew by the look on Meshia's face that this wasn't going to be good. "I know you heard me Durrell, who the fuck is she, and why are you dancing with her?" Nikki said, glaring at me as I turned around. Blocking her view of Meshia, "Nikki, what are you doing here? And you need to lower your voice." Nikki tried to push past me to get to Meshia, "Lower my voice? Are you shitting me? My baby daddy and man is here with another bitch, and you want to know what I am doing here. You invited me, Durrell. Remember, this has been planned for months." "Shit," I said as I continued to block Nikki from Meshia. "Shit. Well, being that we broke up, I didn't think that offered still stood," I said, glaring at her. Damn, I wanted to choke the shit out of her for being this shitty, especially in front of Meshia. Before I could move out of the way, Meshia stepped from behind me and said, "Durrell, I am going to excuse myself to the lady's room and grab a drink. I will let you handle your business in private. "Meshia, wait," I said, trying to grab her arm before she walked away, but she walked past me fast. "No, go ahead. Come find me when you're done," she said with a disappointed smile on her face. Before I could get another word in, she disappeared into the crowd of onlookers. I turned back around to face Nikki, who had a smirk on her face and her arms folded across her chest. "This is not the place or time to discuss the fact I already told your ass we were done. Go home, and I will call you tomorrow." "The hell you will. I don't trust that either. You meet me at my place in one hour, ready to talk about our future or I will run to every tabloid that will listen to your little secret," Nikki said, looking me right in my eyes. My heart was pounding, and I could feel the tension from clutching my jaw so straight. "You wouldn't dare," I said as I forcefully grabbed her arm, leading her to the back patio and away from the crowd and music. "We agreed that we would never speak about THAT." "Well, I changed my mind, and if you don't do exactly what I want, I will tell everything I know and let go of my arm; you are hurting me," Nikki said, trying to pull from my grasp. I held on tighter and pulled her closer to me. "Are you threatening me, Nikki? You sure you want to go there with me?" "Hmm, now there's my man. Hmm, just have that same energy later when you get to my place. I released her arm and gently pushed her towards the door. "One Hour, Durrell! One Hour!" Nikki said as she walked out the door. "Shit," I said to myself, turning around to head to the bar. I needed a drink and to figure out what excuse I could give to Meshia for having to leave.

MESHIA

I looked at myself in the bathroom mirror, rinsing my mouth because I had just thrown up in the toilet. I had felt nauseous as soon as Durrell and I hit the dance floor. It must have been from the champagne we had on the way over in the limo. I couldn't believe that I was at the mayor's ball with Durrell of all people, in the latest Gucci dress and my hair slew by Ty B, the best beautician in the business. I felt like I was walking on air until that want-to-be barbie reject came trying to lay claim. Shit, I thought he was done with her since he was pursuing me. I knew that Nigga was too good to be true. I turned on the water and ran a napkin under it and placed it on my neck to help calm myself down. The door to the bathroom opened, and before I knew it, I felt a hand on the small of my back and another over my mouth. "What the," I tried to mouth out, looking into the mirror to see Markus standing behind me with a crazy look in his eyes. "It is me, Mesh," he said, letting go of me but blocking the entrance to the bathroom. "Have you lost your God damn mind? How the fuck did you know I was in here?" I asked, moving back away from him whilst looking him in his face. The smell of his cologne had me wanting to throw up all over again. "I saw you come in here, and I saw you come in with Durrell," he said, slurring his words. What are you doing with him, Mesh?" "First off, I don't answer to you, and second you're drunk. Get out of the way, Markus,"

I said, taking a step towards the door. "Why are you here with HIM of all people? What does he have that I don't Mesh?" He said, moving towards me. "Well, for starters, a wife. Markus, move out of my way and leave me alone." I tried to push past him, but he was too strong. He grabbed my arms and pushed me against the nearest wall, pinning my arms. "Mesh, all I have ever wanted was you. How many times do I have to tell you that I am sorry? You were never supposed to find out about Tracie," Markus whined. "Speaking of your wife, where is she tonight, and what would she say about you being in the lady's bathroom with me?" I said, trying to get out of the hold. The look in his eyes changed, and the soft expression he had on his face turned into one that made the hairs on my head stand up. I started to get scared. "Markus, let me go. Okay, I forgive you, just let me go; you're hurting me. He looked into my eyes and moved down and kissed me roughly. "Markus, stop, let me go, stop, or I will scream," I said, shaking. "Go ahead, you know I like it when you scream." He used his free hand to lift up my dress and ran his hand over the top of my thong. "It feels just like I remember," he said huskily into my ear. "Markus, I said, stop. Are you going to rape me in a lady's bathroom?" His hand stops just before slipping into my thong. "What did you say?" "You heard me. Are you going to rape me, Markus? Cause that's exactly what you will be doing if you don't let me go." He released my arms and backed away from me, stumbling. "Meshia I, I would never hurt you." "Been there and done that, Markus. Get out of here before I call security and tell them what you were almost about to do." He looked up at me and started to walk towards me. I made a dash for the bathroom door and walked out, trying to straighten my dress and stop the tears from streaming down my face. I walked out into the hallway, not watching where I was going. I ran straight into the back of Durrell. "Excuse me, Oh Meshia, I was just locking for you," he said, turning around and looking at me. "What is wrong? What happened? Why are you crying?"

Just then, Markus came out of the bathroom yelling, "Meshia, wait." Durrell looked at Markus and then back at me. "Meshia, what the fuck is going on? Why are you crying?" Markus came up, trying to push past Durrell. "Man, this doesn't have shit to do with you; mind your own business, D."

"SHE is my business, bro, and no disrespect, I wasn't talking to you," Durrell said, shoving Markus, making him stumble back. Before I could say anything, Markus had found his balance and tried to swing on Durrell. Durrell saw what Markus was trying to do, and his fist landed on Markus's right jaw, laying him out on the ground. "I know damn well your ass didn't just try to swing on me," Durrell said as he turned to face me. "Are you ok? Did he hurt you?" He placed his arms around me, and the tears fell. "Baby, please, tell me what's wrong." I pulled back, and the tears kept falling. I looked at him and said, "I am sorry, I have to go." I turned and ran down the hall towards the front entrance before he could run after me.

DURRELL

"Do you want to explain to me what the fuck that was all about?" I said to Markus, who was still on the floor rubbing his right jaw, which was swollen from my punch. "I asked you a fucking question. What did you do to her, and why the fuck were you coming out of the bathroom after her?"

Markus didn't answer and tried to stand up. I moved toward him to hit him again, but my security came rushing in front of me. "You okay, boss," one of them said as they ran up. "Yea, I am good. Put his ass in an Uber to get home," I said, motioning toward Markus, who was trying to get up off the floor but was too drunk and confused from my punch to do so by himself. "Yes, sir," they replied. "I am headed out solo." John, who had been my bodyguard for over ten years, asked, "You sure that's wise," raising his eyebrow. "Yea, I am sure. Meet me back at the house in 3 hours; I got to go handle something." I walked out from one of the side doors to avoid any lingering media. I slid into my limo. "Head over to Nichole's," I told my driver. As I got seated in the back of the limo, I pulled out my phone to call Meshia to make sure she was okay. "Hey, this is Meshia. Leave a message at the beep." "Hey, it's Durrell. I was calling to explain and to see if you were okay. Can you please pick up?

I hung up the phone and sent a text message with the same message. I closed my phone and tried to get ready for whatever Nichole had up her sleeve. Whatever it was, I was going to end it tonight. If I ever want a chance at a future with Meshia, this shit with Nichole had to end.

The limo pulled up to Nichole condo about 30 minutes later. She lived in a high raise midtown Dallas, a place she just begged me that she had to have. I made a mental note to have my assistant stop all payments for her rent. As we pulled up to the front of the building, I poured myself a drink of basil Hayden whiskey and downed it. Letting the whiskey settle in, my driver said, "We are here, sir." I poured myself another shot, trying to get myself ready for whatever game Nichole was about to try and play. "Alright, let's get this shit over with," I said aloud as I got out of the limo and headed into Nichole's building. The whiskey had already started to give me false courage as I rode the elevator to her floor. Before I could even get my key in her door, it flung open, and there she was, standing in the royal blue nighty that I purchased for her while we were in Paris last year. Damn, she looked good. One thing I never had a complaint about was that Nichole always kept herself in shape and looked camera perfect. I swallowed the large lump that had developed in my throat, trying not to focus on her as I walked past her into the condo. She had me a drink already poured on the bar next to the large ceiling to floor windows that gave a great view of the Dallas skyline. I took my drink off the bar and stared out the window, trying to gather my thoughts, when Nichole came up behind me and placed her hand on my chest and her head on my back. I spun around and looked her dead in her eyes and said, "I told you never to bring that shit up

EVER, and you want to go saying it at a public event. Have you lost your fucking mind?" She took a step back, looking hurt but still sexy as hell. "Now, now, let's watch the tone. I only said that because I was hurt. Why would you bring that want-to-be thing to the ball when you knew we were supposed to go together?" I rubbed my hand down my face and said, "Nikki, we been over this. I broke up with you after I caught you fucking my producer in my bathroom in my home. Why would you assume that you would still be invited to anything that has to do with me? She looked even madder as I continued. "You know damn well the only reason you know about "that" is because I was beyond drunk, and it was a conversation you were never supposed to hear; shit, anyone for that matter. You swore that night and even signed the NDA that you would never even hint at that." Nichole held up her hand for me to stop. "Yes, I signed that NDA and agreed to that because I thought we were going to be married and all that. I didn't think that you were going to leave me for some want-to-be Keshia Knight Pullman reject, she whined. Now I wonder what she would think about the fact that you had your fiancée, her lover, and his baby killed. What was her name again? Oh Yes, Jenna. I wonder how your little hood rat would feel knowing you Killed Jenna before she could get the last symbols out." My hands were around her neck choking her. "Say her name again, say it again," I said as I squeezed harder around her neck.... "I would be very careful with the shit you say to me, or you just might end up like them." "Nichole was trying to hit my hands with her arms. Her light brown skin was turning a light shade of blue, but the look in her green eyes showed a hint of pleasure and excitement. I let her go before I killed her, and she dropped to the floor, gasping for air. "Crazy ass. If I didn't know any better, I think you like this crazy ass shit," I said, walking back to the bar to pour myself another drink. I was beginning to feel strange and horny. Nichole got up from the floor and said, "Hmm, you know how much I like it when you choke me." She got on the couch, which was in the middle of the room, and spread her eagle. As I turned around, I saw her dip her manicured fingers into her pussy, in and out, in and out. My dick jumped from in my pants. "Fucking trader," I said to myself as I began to head over to the couch. "Oh, you want me to choke you? Is that what you need? You need me to teach you a lesson?" "Yass Daddy," she said. She inserted her fingers into her pussy and then up to her mouth, sucking off her own juices. Damn, I was fucked. She knew how much that shit turned me on, and with the drinks I had in the limo, I wasn't thinking with sense. She got up from the couch and walked up to me, and undid my pants buckle, allowing my pants to drop to the floor, releasing my throbbing dick.

She dropped to her knees and put my dick into her mouth and started moving it in and out of her mouth. I grabbed a fistful of her hair and pushed it deeper into her mouth. Every stroke I gave her, she let slide deep down her throat, never gagging. That shit felt so good that it made my toes curl. Right, when I was about to burst my load into her mouth, Nichole pulled back, and I slipped out her mouth. She immediately turned around, got on all four legs, doggie style, and I entered her from the back. I began stroking her in a circular motion. She matched every stroke. I put my left leg up on the edge of the couch so I could go deeper. "Hmm baby, shit ...yes harder," Nichole purred. I pumped into her harder and grabbed her neck with both hands starting to choke her. "Yes, baby, harder. Choke me harder." I tightened my grip on her neck and kept pumping, feeling myself getting ready to burst. As I pumped harder, I began to cum, feeling the tingling start at the bottom of my balls, blood rushing straight to my head. I tried to pull out so I could cum on her back, but Nichole clutched her inner walls, keeping my dick locked in place. "Oh shit, shit, oooooh, ooooh," I yelled as my cum shot out. I felt like she was trying to pull every drop of semen out of me. "Yes, baby, oh, oh, D shit," Nichole yelled below me.

I stood dazed for a few seconds as the blood rushed back to my head, and the feeling in my legs and feet came back. I pulled out of her and pushed her forward on the couch and pulled my pants up from around my legs, tucking my dick back in my pants and buckling them up. Nichole looked a little hurt as I began to walk towards the door to leave. "You got what you wanted, Nichole, me fucking you. We are done now, and if you know what is best for you, you will keep your mouth closed. I would hate to see something happen to you suddenly." Before she could even get up to say anything back, I walked out the door, letting it slam. I hustled to the elevator door, which was opened as soon as I got into the hallway, in case Nichole wanted to make a scene. Once I was in the elevator, I tried to piece together what I had just done. The fact I had just nutted in her raw was making my stomach hurt. "You will be fine; she is on birth control," I said aloud to myself. "Shit. At least I hope she still is." I pulled out my phone from my pocket to text my driver and noticed I had a missed call from Meshia. "Meshia, shit." How the fuck could I explain to her how I just fucked Nichole. As the elevator reached the ground, I dialed back Meshia's number, but it went straight to voice mail again. I hung up without leaving a message. I needed to get my mind right before I tried to speak with her. I slid into the limo and still couldn't believe what had just happened.

NICHOLE

What the fuck... that is not how I thought this was going to go. I thought he would have at least spent the night. "Fuck this heffa; whoever she is, has D's mind all messed up," I said, still looking at the door he had just left out of. "Fuck that hoe, remember the plan," one of the voices in my head said. "Oh, shit, you are right," I said aloud, rushing to my bedroom. I hopped on my bed and put a pillow under my butt, and put my legs up in the air, resetting them above my headboard. I had read in last May issue of Women's health that you have a better chance of getting your egg fertilized after sex if you lay in this position for 30 minutes, and shit, I needed all the help I could get if I was going to pull this whole my baby daddy stunt off. I slid my laptop over onto the top of my stomach and almost forgot that I had my web camera rolling the whole time. "Durrell was here," I giggled out loud because I couldn't believe that I got him on camera fucking me and also basically admitting murdering or at least admitting to involvement in his Ex's, her lover, and their child's murder. That was a story for a different day. The details I learned about that night were something even too devilish for me. I mean, I was all about getting what I wanted, but I don't' think I would ever go as far as to having someone killed. "GO best friend, that's my Best Friend." "Your better, you better, my phone started ringing. "Damn, where is my phone?" I felt around the bed, looking for it, trying not to move since I still had at least twenty minutes left to give Durrell's little swimmers a better chance. I finally found it under one of my massive body pillows. I answered right before the last ring. "Hey, T." Before I could even get out another word, Tracie said, "He still isn't home. I am tired of this shit," she said with sadness in her voice. "T, we have been over this. You know that you deserve better," I said, rolling my eyes. We had been over this conversation so many times. I did mean half of what I said. Tracie did deserve better. She had been a good friend, and she was the mother to my God twins, but she was just going to have to be a causality of this war I was raging on everyone. "I know, I know. That's why I am calling. I need your help with something, and it can't be talked about over the phone. It has to be face to face." "Hmm, okay. I can be over first thing in the morning," I said. "No, I can't talk about it here at the house. Meet me at the Starbucks at North Park around 9 am," she said as I heard one of my God twins crying in the background. "I got to go; the boys woke up." "Okay, I will see you tomorrow, and "T," "Yeah," she said. "I meant what I said. You and the boys deserve better." "I know Nik, believe me I know," she said softly. "I will see you tomorrow and Thank you." She hung up before I could say anything else. "Well, this just got even more interesting," I said aloud. "I wonder what she wants my help with. I definitely hope it's not about Markus and me." "Now, how would she have found that out?" One of the voices in my head said. "I don't know; we do a great job at covering our tracks with that," I said back. "Exactly, so stay focused on your plans and worry about what she has to say later," the louder voice in my head said. "Right, Right. Stay focused," I said, repositioning the pillow under my butt for better comfort and started to feel sleepy. I can't wait to see the look on Durrell's face when the pregnancy test showed positive in a few weeks. Shit, it better work after all the work I had just put in.

TRACIE

I was pissed and sad that I thought for one second that this Negro would come home after a party. I mean, I don't know why I thought shit would be different now that the twins and I were home. I rolled over to Markus's side of the bed, which had not been slept in. This is a feeling I know all too well, night after night waking up alone; it was getting old. I couldn't believe that I had become "that" female who stayed with a man who continuously disrespected her by cheating and lying. There had been so many times I just looked the other way as Markus did what he wanted. I sat up in bed with tears starting to stream down my face. All the years I spent trying to be the best wife I could, playing my part as the wife of the great awarding winner producer Markus Darrius Damon. I used to tell myself how lucky I was to be his wife and the position I was in. That was all out the window the moment all his bullshit almost cost me my babies and my life. That is where I drew the line. I pulled on my robe, climbed out of bed, grabbed the baby monitor off the nightstand, and headed to the twins' room. As I opened the door, Darius, the smaller of the twins, began to coo as I walked into the room and turned on the table light. Travis, the larger of the boys, was still sound asleep. I picked up Darrius and positioned myself in the rocking chair so that I could breastfeed him. "Little man, your bother, and you are my life. I promise I am going to do what I have to make sure we are good." He quickly latched on to my right nipple. As he fed, I started to think about my next move and how I was going to get out of this marriage with everything without it looking planned. "Hmm, Think Tracie, think," and after about 10 minutes, it came to me as I burped Darrius. "The best way to catch a fish is with bait," I said aloud, waking up Travis. I changed Darius and laid him back into his crib and picked up Travis to feed him. "Perfect," I said to myself. "Hurry up, little man, momma needs to go secure some bait for your bitch ass daddy."

About two hours later, it was about 8:50 AM before I got finished feeding, changing the twins' diapers, and getting dressed. I had called my mom to come over and sit with the boys while I met up with Nichole to discuss my plan. I prayed she would agree to it because I couldn't trust anyone else with what I was planning. I was sitting at one of the tables at Starbucks when I saw Nichole walking up, looking like she had just gotten off a runway show. She always had herself together. Damn, I was always jealous of that fact. She never gained a pound. "Hey, bestie," she said as she sat down. "Hey girl, thanks for meeting me," I said as I took a sip of my Tazo Peach Tranquility Tea. I wished I could get my normal Carmel Macchiato upside down, but I couldn't have caffeine with breastfeeding the boys. "How are my God babies doing," Nichole said. "I need to come over to see them." "Yes, you do. So how was the mayor's ball?" I said, trying to make small talk before I just jumped in on what I needed her to do.

"It was interesting enough. I saw Markus there," she said. "I will be right back; I am going to go and get a coffee." I was about to reply when a hand touched my shoulder, causing me to turn around. "Ms.

Damon?" I knew that voice as I had heard it many times while in my coma. I almost memorized it. "Dr. Bryant," I said, turning around with a big smile. "Hi, how are you?" "I am doing well. I was just out running some errands and saw you sitting here and wanted to say hello, and to remind you to call and schedule your follow up appointment with my office," he said, showing off his perfectly shaped white teeth and handsome smile with his dimples showing. "Call me Tracie. I most definitely plan to schedule that soon," I said, flashing him my sexiest smile. We must have been staring at each other for a while until Nichole cleared her throat and came back to the table with her drink. "And who is this handsome specimen?" She said. "Oh," I said. "Nichole, this is Dr. Bryant. He treated me while I was in the hospital." "Pleasure to meet you," Dr. Bryant said, looking a little uncomfortable. "Well, Ms. Dam... I mean Tracie, I look forward to seeing you soon. If you will excuse me, I need to get going." He walked off but not without looking back, giving me another killer view of his gorgeous smile. "What was that all about?" Nichole said, looking at me. "What was what?" I said, taking a sip of my now room temperature tea. "Just my doctor." "Just your Doctor huh, that is one hot doctor," Nichole said with a smirk. "If I didn't know any better, I would say that he was trying to flirt with you." "Girl, please, lol, that's all in your mind," I said, blushing. "Yeah, okay, so enough stalling; why don't you tell me what you need my help with, and why all the secrecy?" I looked up at her and looked her straight in her green eyes, "I need you to sleep with my husband."

MARKUS

"Hey Markus, wake up." I felt someone shaking me out of my sleep. "Leave me alone Tracie, it's too early," I said, rolling over to go back to sleep. "Who the fuck is Tracie," said the unfamiliar voice, not matching that of my wife's. "It is not too early; it is after 1 pm." I turned over, startled to see that I was not at home in my bed, but I was in one of the bedrooms in my uptown studio. I looked at the stranger, who was about 5'7. She had 24-inch blonde extensions, a small waist, and a big 40DDD cup breast that were exposed. The events of last night all came rushing back to me as I sat up in bed. "Julie, is your name, right?" I said to her. "No, my name is Julissa," she said, looking mad and offended as she started looking for her clothes. "Right, Julissa. I am sorry, baby," I said, pulling her back down on the bed. "Let me make it up to you." She pulled out my arms and said, "No. Why don't you call Tracie, whoever that is instead?" She hopped up and put on the rest of her clothes and headed out the door. I laid back on the bed, sighing. "Shit, Tracie." I started looking for my phone on the dresser next to me. She was going to have my head and dick on a platter since I didn't come home. I knew she had called my phone over a hundred times because all the missed call notifications came through as soon as I powered it up. Knock Knock. "Markus, D is here for his studio session; you have 15 mins," my assistant said through the door. "Alright, I will be up in a few minutes," I yelled, laying down in the bed. I turned my phone back off. Shit, no point in stressing about how many ways Tracie was probably going to kill me once I got home. Right, I had to go upstairs and play nice with Durrell to see how serious things were with him and Meshia. Shit, he was my main artist, and I need this album to do crazy numbers. I got up and headed to the bathroom. By the time I got out of the shower, I was ready to get this face to face with Durrell.

MARKUS

Once I got upstairs to my studio, I saw Durrell's typical crew outside, eating on some fruit and veggie trays. I entered into the sound room where Durrell was already in the booth, working on his latest track, "For the Love of it All." It was a slow ballet that would be sure to debut at number one on the billboard. I gave him a head nod and sat down in my seat, watching Lucas, my sound technician, leveling out the background vocals. I noticed that he didn't give the usual head nod back. Well, I knew this was going to be one hell of a session. About 30 minutes later, Durrell came out of the booth, and we were all sitting listening to the playback of the entire song. "Think we need to double the vocals at the end of the track so that it sounds a little better," I said to Durrell, who was sitting across the room. He said nothing but just kept looking at me with a glare. "D, did you hear me?" Knowing damn well he heard me; I looked at him directly. "No, I think it sounds fine the way it is," he said with an attitude. "Hey, I need the room cleared right now. Everyone out but D and me," I said, getting up from my chair. It was time to have this showdown because I will be damned if he messes up this track cause he is in his feeling over Meshia. Shit. As far as I am concerned, he isn't hers to have an attitude over. She will forever be mine, well, at least in my mind. Everyone got up and dabbed up D. I walked over to the door to the studio and closed it. Before I could turn around, Durrell came from behind me and pinned me to the door, grabbing my arm so that my chest and face were trapped in between the door and him. "You want to tell me what the fuck you did to Meshia at the ball? I swear if you did anything to her, I am going to kill you," he snarled. "You need to calm the fuck down, Durrell. I did not do shit to Meshia." I tried to get him to release his grip, but he held firm. "Do not lie to me. How do you even know her," he yelled. "Like I said, you need to calm the fuck down and let go of my arm, and I can tell you what happened," I said. He let me go and walked over to the studio bar to pour a drink. "I am waiting," he said as he took a sip of his drink. I fixed my clothes and walked to the other side of the room and sat in my chair and took a deep breath for this lie I was about to tell. "Man, I do not know her. I was super drunk and thought it was the men's bathroom." I looked up at him to see if he was buying what I was saying. He took another drink and continued to glare at me. "So, when I saw shorty in there, I must have scared her, and I tried to get her to calm down. When I recognized her from the party a few weeks ago, she freaked out and ran out, and that's when you came and punched the shit out of me," I said, still looking at him trying to sound as convincing as possible by rubbing my jaw which was still sore. "Oh, okay, I guess that does make sense. Your ass was super drunk. You must not have meant to go into the women's bathroom," he said, taking another swig of his drink and relaxing a little bit. I exhaled a little bit. "Yeah, I am actually really embarrassed. Your ass did not have to punch me, though," I said. "My bad," he said. "I just panicked when I saw her crying like that. It freaked me out," he said. "So, you and shorty got something going on?" I said as I walked over to the bar for a drink. I was going to need

I woke up feeling like I had to throw up, luckily, I had my trash can right next to the couch. I spent all night there crying my eyes out. I had cried so hard that I made myself throw up a few times. Just the thought of last night had my stomach in more knots. I leaned over the trash can and heaved serval times before I threw up. I tried to stand up to go to the bathroom to shower, but another wave of nausea came over me. I laid back down on the couch and closed my eyes, trying not to think about what almost happened last night. Before I knew it, I had drifted off to sleep, and when I woke up, it was well into the evening. I slowly got up from the couch and stood. When I didn't feel any nausea, I walked to the bathroom and took off my clothes. I stared at myself in the mirror. I must be coming down with something because my brown skin looked very greyish. As I turned on the shower, I made a mental note to call my doctor on Monday. I stayed in the shower for what seemed to be about an hour. By the time I got out, the water had run cold, but I was feeling much better. I walked into my bedroom drying off, laid across my bed, grabbed my phone, and turned it on. I had turned it off as soon as I got home from the party last night. I had a few messages from my staff asking questions about tonight's service, a message from Renee asking me how the ball went last night. I'm going to call her as soon as I got in. I had a few missed calls from Durrell and one voice message. I stared at the void. I stared at my phone, thinking whether or not I was going to play it. I didn't know what I was going to say to him about running out last night. I didn't even know if I wanted to face him, especially after seeing that made up Barbie doll that said that she was his. "OK, Meshia, get it together; it's just a voicemail. It's not that big of a deal. It's not like I have to call him back," I told myself. I pressed play on the voicemail message, and Durrell's smooth baritone voice filled my room. "Uhh, hey Meshia, this is Durrell. Well, I guess you know that since you can see my name calling. Yeah, uhh, I was checking to make sure you were ok. You were really upset when you rushed out last night; I just wanted to make sure you were okay. Please give me a call when you get this or if you feel up to it." Just his voice alone made me want to melt. I couldn't explain why that is. We haven't even known each other for long. "But that didn't stop you from jumping his bones the very first time you met him," I thought. I sat on my bed for what seemed to be forever before I decided to call him back. My hands were shaking as I pressed his name, and the phone began to ring. The phone rang three times before he answered in a sleepy voice, "Hello."

"Hi, uhh, it is Meshia. Did I wake you?" I said, biting my lip nervously. "No, No, I was hoping you would call back. I called you a few times last night, are you ok? You rushed out last night so quick." I swallowed a big lump that had seemed to form in my throat, trying to think of a lie I was about to tell him. "Oh yeah, I am so sorry I ran out like that, I wasn't feeling well, so I went to the bathroom and entered that random guy into the bathroom." "Did he hurt you? I swear if he did, I will...." He said, getting upset. "No, he didn't," I interrupted him. "I was just in the wrong bathroom; I am completely fine." I looked up at my ceiling with tears threatening to fall. I was far from being ok. "Well, I am sorry we didn't get a chance to have a better time; I was really looking forward to spending more time with you." "I was too; I am so sorry again. I promise I will make it up to you." "You mean that?" He said with excitement in his voice. "Yes, I mean it," I said with a chuckle. "Prove it. Come with me to New Orleans." I sat up and said, "Wait, what? You are not serious." "Yes, I am dead serious. I have a set at the Essence in a few days and would love the company. We can chill and see the city before the concert. What do you say?" He asked. I sat in silence, looking at my phone, not sure what to say. I could use the distraction and going on a trip with a handsome man in a city with good food, possibly could be what I needed. "So, what do you say?" Durrell asked. I let out the breath I was holding. "Okay, yes, I will go." "Great, I will text you the details. I promise you; this will be a weekend you won't forget." I smiled and said, "I am sure it will be." "Well, I hate to cut this short. I have to head to the studio, but I will give you a call later on."

"Okay," I said, "Talk to you soon." I hung up the phone and laid back on my bed, staring at the ceiling. What the fuck was I getting myself into.

NICHOLE

I sat across, looking at Tracie like she had lost her mind like I really felt like she had lost her mind. "Wait, back up. You want me to do what?" I said to her while taking a sip of my coffee. "I want you to sleep with my husband," she repeated even more calmly than before. "I heard what you said the first time Tracie, what the fuck?" She looked around as to see if anyone was watching or listen. "Look okay. So, before I had the twins, I found out that Markus was cheating on me, and still is. And let's be real, he has been cheating for years, and I have had enough. I want out, but I want something for all the years of pain." I looked at her, shocked that she was actually saying this. I was interested to see how serious she really was. "And T, what exactly is it that you want?" I asked. "I want EVERYTHING," she said with an evil grin. I want to take away everything that Markus holds dear, but I need you to complete that. Before I could respond, my phone lit up with a text message from Markus saying, "Get your ass to the condo, NOW."

I clicked the phone off and looked at Tracie and said, "Whatever you need me to do, you know I got your back, bestie. What's the plan?" She smiled and said, "I knew I could count on you."

Little did she know I was one of the reasons she was so unhappy, but I feel like this is my way to set things back in the balance between her and me. I mean, she is my best friend, even though I had been sleeping with her husband; I mean, he was mine, to begin with. I picked my phone up and texted Markus back: "OMW."

TRACIE

I couldn't believe that I really just asked my best friend to sleep with my husband. Like, what the fuck is wrong with me. But shit, I couldn't think of any other way to get out of this marriage with Markus. How else? How else was I supposed to get out of this marriage? I mean, he had everything. The cars are in his name, the house is in his name, and the only person I could trust was Nikki. I mean, let's be real, she's a hoe. She was always known to sleep around since we were kids, and something tells me this isn't the first time she would have been doing something like this. All I needed was just either a videotape or a picture of Markus cheating, and then based on the prenup, I would get everything. He thought he was so slick putting that clause in the Prenup, thinking that I wasn't going to see it. He even put in there that if I was caught cheating, he would get all of my assets, including the trust fund that my grandfather left for me and custody of any future children we had. Well, I'm tired. I deserve better. My kids deserve better. Thanks to him, I could have lost them and my life that night.

As I pulled up to the house, I was praying and hoping that Markus wouldn't be there. I pressed the button on the garage door opener, thankful when I didn't see his car in his space. As I got out of the car and entered the house, I thought back to the plan that I had made with Nikki at lunch. It was foolproof. All she had to do was get Markus drunk at the studio, telling him that she needed to talk to him about a surprise party that she wanted to throw for my birthday, and all she had to do was get him drunk enough to want to fuck. I mean, it wouldn't take much. This is Markus we're talking about. She didn't even have to go all the way through with fucking him; she just had to make it good enough so that the studio cameras would pick it up, and then the problem is solved. "Hey mom, I'm back," I called out to my mother, who had been watching the Twins for me. "Hey, honey," my mom said as she walked in with both of my boys in her arms. "Did you have a nice lunch?" I walked over to her, replying, "Oh, it was definitely life-changing," as I grabbed one of the boys from her, cuddling him to my face, taking in a deep breath of the baby scent. "Well, that's good, honey. I'm going to go lay the boys down for a nap before I take off so you can get some rest." Thanks, mom," I said to her, sitting down on the couch. "I appreciate it." My mom walked back into the back bedroom where the boys nursery was, and then my phone rang. I picked it up to see if it would be Markus, but it was a text message from an unknown number saying, "Hey Tracie, this is DOC. I wanted to see if you were free for those drinks?" I smiled and replied, "Yes, sure, how does six o'clock sound?" I set my phone down as I waited for the text to replied. Buzz Buzz. my phone went off a few seconds later. "Yes, that would be perfect replied," DOC. "How's the embassy suites downtown sound?" I replied back. "Sounds great. See you then." I put my phone back down and rushed to the boys' nursery to ask my mom if she could stay a little while longer, and she replied, "Sure, honey, you know I love spending time with my grandkids." I smiled and said, "Thanks, mom. You're a lifesaver," as I walked out of the room and headed to my bedroom to get dressed. "What's the harm in a few drinks," I said to myself. "Shoot, maybe Markus won't be the only one getting some play tonight," I chuckled, knowing damn well I wouldn't do anything to jeopardize my plan. I stopped as I walked past my full-length mirror and looked at myself. I felt butterflies in my stomach and a headache coming on. While I was out drinking with my doctor, my best friend would be fucking my husband. Shake it off, shake it off, shake it off T, as I walked to my bathroom to turn on the shower. It won't be long now before you have everything you deserve. That bitch ass husband of mine gets everything he deserves.

NICHOLE

I don't know why I am so nervous about meeting up with Markus. I mean, it's not like I haven't been fucking him for years, but this felt different. Tracie asking me to do it and to prove it seems even wrong for me. I figured that I could probably get away with just getting him to do oral, and that should be enough to pacify her, and whatever it was she needed with these pictures. I had a bad feeling as I pulled the mirror down on my car visor. Beep, Beep, my phone went off as I applied my lipstick again. I picked up my phone, put my passcode in, and saw a message that read, "Blood test came back positive" from an unknown number. I knew who that message came from, and I let out a loud squeal. "Oh, my fucking God, I can't believe it worked. It freaking worked." As I said that, a wave of nausea came over me. It finally set in. "Oh crap, I'm pregnant, I'm freaking pregnant. A second text message came in through my phone. It read, "Are you there? Did you do it already?" From Tracie. I was so busy with the previous text messages that I forgot that I was sitting in front of Markus's condo and what I was about to do. I wanted to drive immediately to D's place to tell him that he was going to be a daddy, but the voice said, "No girl, remember the plan. Stay focused. You will have plenty of time for D to play baby daddy." I sighed and said out loud, "Yea, you right." I freshened my makeup and reached for my phone. I texted Tracie, "No, not yet. Just got here. I will let you know when it is done." I hit send and got out of my car and headed towards Markus's condo. I noticed that his car was not in the driveway as I pulled in. I entered the pin into the keypad. "He must have parked in the garage," I said to myself as I opened the door. "Markus, you home," I called out as I walked through the door, closing it behind me. I was met with silence as I made my way to the back of the condo to look for him in the home studio where he often was. "Nope, not in there," I said as I peeked in to see no one there. "Markus," I shouted out again, still silent. I pulled out my tracking app to see if I could see where he was. I had tracking on him too. It showed him at some residence location in Arlington, Texas. Shit, he's not even here, probably at some other hoe's house. Well, might as well be nosey," I said. I headed up the stairs to his office to see what I could find. I had known Markus enough to know where he kept all the keys to his desk and knew him well enough to know what the possible codes could be to his computer. As I entered the room, I looked around and saw all the award plaques that Markus has won for working with various artists. I stopped in front of Durrell's first platinum album plaque and placed my hand on my stomach, "I hope you're talented like your daddy." My phone buzzed, scarring the shit out of me. "What's going on? Did it happen?"- T. I shook my head. "Ugh, why is she trying to rush me," I said, putting my phone back in my bag. Even if I was to fuck Markus, it must definitely not be rushed," I chuckled, moving towards his desk. I pulled back the big office chair and sat down. I wasn't sure what I was looking for, but I knew Markus probably had some shit laying around that I could use. If I were Markus, where would I hide my dirt? Markus is not the average cheating man; he wouldn't just leave anything on his computer for Tracie to come and find or any other person. So checking his computer would be a waste of time. Think Nick; he is old school. There were many times I remembered Markus pulling out his old camera and taking pictures of me before, during, and after sex. "Hmm... now where would he hide all those?" I started to move the different items on his desk to see if I could find a key for his desk drawers. I was sure that it wouldn't be that easy or that he wouldn't be that obvious, but as I moved the plant vase off his desk, there was a key. I take that back that he would be smarter to hide stuff from Tracie.

I grabbed the key and tried the first desk drawer, no fit ... I moved to the second and third and no luck; I sat back in the chair, looking around the room, and noticed on a bookshelf a built-in cabinet. I got up and put the key into the cabinet lock and turned, "Let this be something," I said as I opened the door. Inside was a bunch of files with names on them, Nichole (me on top), Justice S., Carleta P., and a bunch more. I opened a few to see that my thought on Markus's obsession with taking photos of who he was fucking was right on. I sifted through a free more file folders until one name caught my attention, Meshia. I opened the file to see if it was who I thought it was, and "Bingo," I said. "This is too good to be true," I said. Inside the folder were over 100 pictures of Markus and Meshia in various sexual positions. "Damn, that hoe is flexible." I couldn't believe that I had such great luck; these pictures would serve all purposes. I took my phone out and began snapping shots of some of the pictures of Markus and some of the other girls and sent them with a message to Tracie, "Job done." I was getting ready to take some pictures of Markus and Meshia's photos when the voice said, "These photos will be much better served direct." I smiled, "You are so right." I decided to take my folder out of the stack along with Meshia's file folder, no reason to leave a trail about Markus and me. I put everything back into the cabinet, locked it and returned the key to its place under the flower vase. I made sure to straighten everything on the desk, and just as I was walking out of his office and putting both file folders into my purse, the front door alarm chirped, and in walked Markus.

MARKUS

As I walked into my condo, I saw Nichole inside, not shocked at all that she would be here, being that I first purchased the condo so she and I would have a place to fuck. "What up, Nicki?" I said as I placed my keys down on the hall table, walking towards the living room. "Come here." I knew she must have wanted some dick since she blew my phone up about coming over. Shit and after the studio session and Tracie acting weird as fuck, I definitely could use some sex. "What's up, Nikki?" I said as I entered my living room, taking a seat next to her on my brown leather couch. "Nothing much," she said as she sat on the couch. "You look stressed." She caressed my knee, inching her way up, her hand stopping just above my zipper. "Why don't you let me help you relax?" Sliding my zipper down, my dick jumped as soon as she places her finger around my shaft, pulling it from my pants. She moved her hands up and down, growing it to the full ten inches. Nikki took her mouth on the tip, licked around in a circle a few times. "Oh, damn, Nik, I said as I shifted to get more comfortable. She then moved down, licking my shaft and then putting it in her mouth till it reached the back of her throat. Nikki had always been willing to deep throat my dick, unlike Tracie, who barely even touched it at all. She always turned her nose up at it. One time, she threw up just from barely licking the tip of it. Slurp, Slurp, was the sound of Nikki sucking and gulping my dick that it made me look down to focus on her. She was just a gorgeous woman, always had a nice body. Her tits were firm and perky, about a Double D, and her small waist complimented her big ass. Things probably could have worked between us if she had not been so crazy and evil. Nikki had some real mental issues, but I guess anyone would with the childhood she had. Being sold to the highest bidder by your own doped-up mother would have made anyone crazy. I was brought back to focus when I felt a tingling in my toes and at the base of my balls. I knew and loved this feeling. "Shit, Shit, Shit," I grunted as I began to pump harder into her mouth. She gagged a little but never broke the rhythm of the punishment my dick was doing to her throat. All the blood came rushing to my head as I could feel my load getting ready to flood into her mouth. I pumped as hard and fast as I could into her mouth, placing my hand on the back of her head, so I could pump as far down her throat as my dick would go. "Yes, yes, I am about to cum," I said, dropping my load into her mouth. She swallowed every drop and held on until I did my last pump down the back of her throat. Slumping over and trying to enjoy the feel of the rush I had just gotten, "Damn," I said as I pushed Nikki off me so I could get up from the couch to get a drink from my bar. "That's exactly what I needed, pulling my pants up and zipping up. "You can let yourself out," I said to Nikki as I pulled out a glass and Hennessey and began pouring myself a drink. Nikki was wiping her mouth with a towel from her purse, always prepared, it seemed for moments like this. "Damn, Markus, you can't even offer me a drink. I literally just sucked your soul out of you," she said with an attitude. "I have to get home to Tracie and the twins. You know what it is when you come over here, so don't even try that bullshit on me," I said, taking a few sips of my drink. "You know what, whatever, Markus." she said as she grabbed her purse and headed for the door. "Next time you feel like getting your dick sucked, don't text or call me." She walked out the door and slammed it so hard the picture frame of Tracie and the twins came crashing to the floor. "Damn, crazy-ass hoe," I said, shaking my head, heading to my bathroom so I could clean up. I pulled out my phone and texted, "Roslyn, hey can you come over and clean the apartment." "Yes, sir. I'll be right over, and I will wear your favorite outfit, nothing," she replied. I smiled back at the text I had received from my maid. "Shit, few hours won't hurt since I had been gone this long," I said aloud to myself as I got into the shower. "I will stop and pick up some flowers and crab legs. Tracie will be fine once she sees that." I stood in the middle of my shower and let the double shower head do its work. Little did I know my whole world was crashing down at home.

I couldn't have gotten out of there so fast; if it killed me. I thought I was about to get caught when he walked in. Shit, the only thing I could think of without having him think anything was strange was to either suck his dick or fuck him. Since I wasn't trying to mess up my plans, I chose to suck his dick, not like it was a horrible task. Markus's dick always smelled and tasted clean. That nigga was a stickler for hygiene. I need to figure out how to use this information about Meshia and Markus to my best advantage with Durrell. The text message on my phone went off, and I knew it was Tracie. "CALL ME" – T. "Shit, Sorry girl," I said to myself, "I have bigger issues to handle. Starting with telling my baby daddy he is about to be a daddy." I cranked up my car, but before I could pull out, the wave of nausea got worse; now, I opened up my car door and immediately threw up. I had never been so happy to throw up in my life. This was a sign that confirmed the text message. I wiped my mouth with the back of my hand and put the car in drive. I reached for my phone as I was driving, so I could look at the tracker app that I had put on Durrell's phone to see if he was going to be home when I saw that his location tracker read unknown, and his last location was the studio. I headed in that direction. It took me about 20 minutes to get to the studio from Markus' condo. I got out and headed straight in. I put my code in, but the buzzer said incorrect code. I pressed the code again, and it said incorrect code. As I was getting ready to press it again to make sure that it was not wrong, out came a security guard named Franklin, blocking the entrance. "Excuse me, can I help you?" I looked at him and said, "Yeah, I'm trying to get into the studio, but the code isn't working, which is strange." I walked up to the door and waited for him to open it. He said with a blank stern look, "Can I get your name and ID." I was starting to get annoyed because he knows my damn name, as many times I have come up here to see Durrell. He has got to be joking. "My name is Nichole. Franklin, you know my name." "Sorry, ma'am, I am just following protocol, and everyone has to show ID to get into the building if you don't have your code," he said, still blocking the door. Sigh. "Okay, one second." I looked into my purse and pulled out my wallet, and handed him my ID. "Happy Now?" "Please wait here; I will go scan your ID and make sure you are authorized to enter the building." "Authorized?" I said and rolled my eyes as he walked back into the studio entrance. Since when did Durrell have so much security to get into the studio? This had to have something to do with his new little hoe. "Calm down," the voice in my head said. "Deep Breath. You can't get so worked up now that it's the baby and us." "You are right," I said, letting out a sigh, starting to feel a wave of nausea coming over me. Franklin came back out just as I thought I was going to throw up all over the studio floor. "I am sorry, ma'am, I can't let you into the building; your authorization has been removed, and we are under extreme directions not to let you into the building," he said, smirking a little. "Excuse me, what the fuck did you just say?" As I walked up to him and got in his face. "I know you fucking lying; there is no way DURRELL BABBS would lock me out of his studio."

"Ma'am, please calm down and leave the premises. If you don't, we will have to remove you, and I don't want to have to do that. I am just doing my job," Franklin said, starting to feel uncomfortable with me all in his space. Yelling as loud as I could, "Just get Mr. Babbs on the phone and let him know that Nichole is here and isn't leaving until I speak with him." "Ma'am, I can't do that. Mr. Babbs isn't even here; he is headed to New Orleans for a performance at the Essence Festival. Please leave; I am asking nicely; I will get your message to him that you stopped by," Franklin said, still blocking the entrance to the studio. The nausea began to set in even worse as everything began to set in. This nigga thought he was slick. He had lost his mind if he thought locking me out of his stupid studio would stop me from getting to him. "No, that is not necessary. I will leave. Thank you for your assistance," I said as I walked quickly away, heading back to the parking lot, to my car. Just as I made it to my car, I threw up all over the gravel. "This nigga thinks he is so smart. He must have left his phone at the studio on purpose, which is why the tracking app showed him there." I tried to breathe in deep to stop myself from continuous gagging. "Calm down and regroup... you always did enjoy a weekend in New Orleans," a different voice in my head said." I smirked a little and stood up slowly, placing my hand over my stomach, rubbing it in a circular motion. "Come on, Peanut, let's go find your Daddy." I got into my car, pulled out my phone, and called my travel agent. "Mo, I need the next flight out to New Orleans." I cranked my car up and headed to Dallas International Airport.

DURRELL

I didn't care about what Nichole wanted. I was hoping she would have found someone else by now, or that NFL Player I paid to distract her would have worked for a while. I needed and wanted my full attention on spending time with Meshia. The moment she walked into my music room that day of my party, she has been like a drug, and I have been addicted since. Watching the pure enjoyment on her face from hearing me singing and playing the piano was something I hadn't witnessed from someone in a while. The feeling it gave me, I hadn't felt it since I was five years old and heard Mahalia Jackson singing "Go Tell It On The Mountain." It was my first time trying to sing and hit every note correctly. I had been looking for that feeling that rush, since my first album. Feeling that without evening knowing Meshia's name was something profound. I felt it every time she was near me. It was out of my character to do something as reckless as going in a stranger raw, but I just wanted that feeling to last, such last letters out of her seemed like the best way to do it at the time, or I could have just been really horny from weeks of not having any sex because of my studio schedule. And since that night, it's like I crave wanting that feeling all day like I literally will do everything I can to keep Meshia in my life, and if that meant taking down anyone, I would do it at all costs. I mean, that's why I spasmed out, that night of the mayor's ball with Markus.

She was making me mad by the minute but keep calm, D, she's right in the next room. Taking a deep breath, Meshia was in the bathroom here at my house, and soon we would be miles from Dallas. New Orleans was good place to put some distance between Nikki and myself. Shit, just to be on the safe side, I needed to hurry up and get Meshia on this plane. I had a bad feeling that at any moment Nichole would pop up and start some shit. Just as I was going to go knock on the bathroom door to see if Meshia was ready, out she walked with nothing but a towel wrapped around her head and waist beads resting on her hips. "Ready to get a move on," I said, crossing the room, embracing her and feeling my dick swelling. "Down boy, I thought to myself as I wrapped my arms around Meshia. I felt like this was going to be one of those last moments of peace in my life for a while. Shoot, with Nikki out there; I knew this feeling was too good to be true, so I held on tighter, baby. "I can't breathe, she said, pushing for my grass. "My bad," I said, loosening my tight grip. "Shit, you just smell so good. I was trying to remember it," she chuckled and went to the suitcase on my bed for clothes. "I'm not going anywhere anytime soon," she said as she slipped into her pants and T-shirt. I really wished that I could believe that, but good shit in my life doesn't last that long, I thought silently. The sound of Meshia closing the suitcase brought me back. "Ready to go, love? She said, I grabbed the Suitcase and held the door open for her. "Well, let's catch a flight."

What was I thinking going to New Orleans with a man I've only known for a few months? Why would I get myself in these situations? I'm praying that he isn't the kind of man who will play with a woman's heart but shoot, I didn't know. I just know what I've seen from him. Because if he knew that I would disappear with my baby and I would never let him know cause another abortion is out of the question, I'm never going to put myself through that ever again. So, if that meant I had to do this on my own, I was willing to do that. I don't even know how I would even start this conversation. Hey, guess what? I'm pregnant with your baby even though we've only known each other for a few months. That's what I get for sleeping with a random person and a celebrity at that. "What are you thinking about so hard over there?" Durrell said to me, sitting in a brown-colored leather seat on the opposite side of his private jet. "You want my honest answer," I said, chuckling. "I always want you to be honest with me, Meshia, no matter what it is," he said, looking me straight in my eyes. "I am thinking of how crazy fast this is all moving, ya know. It feels right, but I mean, we barely know each other," I said, looking out the window, too nervous to look back at him. "I know what you mean, but it does feel right, and I would never hurt you or try to get this close with you if I had any doubts," he said, getting up to sit in the chair next to me and putting his hand on my face moving it to look him directly in his eyes. "Let's just live, baby, just live in this moment right here, in this world we have created." Damn, this man knew how to use words. Sigh, I guess he should be a singer, but shit, what actually did I have to lose? Even if this didn't work out, at least I gained something. I then placed my hand on the side of my belly and started to rub it. "Are you OK?" He asked me, looking down at my hand rubbing my stomach. I immediately stopped and looked up at him and said, "Oh yes, just a little motion sickness, but you're right, let's just live in the moment," I said, trying to distract him. The look of concern stayed on his face, so I took his hand and kissed the back of it and said, "I'm good, babe. I'm well ready to see you on stage, so are you going to perform? His face turned into a smile. "OK, well, let me know if you need anything alright, but man, I'm so excited. I'm going to do my whole first album, a little bit from the second album and from this latest album, it's going to be about an hour and a half show." "That sounds great; I can't wait to see you on stage," I said, glad that changing the subject worked. I wasn't ready for the "I am having your baby conversation. Don't know when I would be ready, but right now definitely isn't that time. The stewardess came out and said, "Mr. Babs, the captain, would like you to know that we're going to begin our descent into New Orleans. Please buckle your seat belts as we prepare for landing." Saved by the Bell was all I could think to myself as I looked out the window and saw the New Orleans skyline. I made the mental note that I would tell Durrell about the baby once we got back to Dallas. No matter his reaction, I was going to keep my baby. I just prayed it was a better response than what happened with Markus.

TRACIE

I couldn't believe the shit I saw in the pictures Nikki sent me. I mean, I knew about Meshia and had even come to terms with it, but this nigga had been cheating on me since we met. Oh, and Nikki thought she was slick leaving out the videos and pictures of her and Markus, but my PI had already sent that over that morning. I could not wait till Markus brought his ass home. When he tries to put his code in at the gate, and it didn't work, the look on his face would be part of the satiation and pettiness energy I was on. I had already had all our joint accounts drained and moved into my personal accounts. He was going to be in for a rude awakening. All the credit cards had been frozen or turned off too. There is no turning back at this point. Everyone had to pay. No, matter what, they had to. I could just take the twins, divorce Markus, and move on, but justice would not be served. I had been through much at the cost of others' selfish actions. While I was in that coma, I had time to think about so many plans to make Markus pay. Now, after seeing the files and pictures Nikki had gotten for me and the PI findings, I had enough to get everything I needed for my plan and then some. Nikki was probably thinking that she was getting off free, but the PI gave me the photos and videos with Markus and her, which she failed to give to me with the other files. The wife is always the one who gets screwed and suffers in a story like this, but not me; I would come out the victor in this story. I wanted what everyone stole from me, which is time, but I had to even out the karma since that was impossible. I was going to be a much bigger bitch than she ever could be. I would be lying if I said I wasn't nervous for this to play out; hopefully, it didn't backfire. "Ms. Damon, He has arrived," one of the new bodyguards my mom had hired said, walking into the living room. "Thank you," I said as my mom and our attorney walked into the room. "Let the show begin."

MARKUS

"What the hell were all these news trucks doing on my street," I thought to myself as I pulled up on the private street that led to the house. A bad feeling started to settle in the closer I got to the front gate. A TMZ truck was parked so close to the gate that they had to move as I honked my horn for them to get out of the way. Click, Click, Click, the cameras went off as the paparazzi must have noticed it was my Audi pulling up. Thank God, I had an illegal tint on my windows. Click, Click, Click, the camera flashes kept going off as I reached for my gate clicker on my visor. I clicked it twice and waited for the gate to open. Click, Click, Click, these cameras were really starting to work my damn nerves. I clicked the clicker again a few more times, and nothing happened; the gate didn't open. "Shit, maybe the batteries were dead," I said as I clicked a few more times before throwing it in the back seat, frustrated. I grabbed my cell from the car holder, and scrolled to Tracie's name, and hit call. Click, Click, Click. "Your call has been routed to T-Mobile," the operator said. "What the fuck," I shouted aloud, hitting my steering wheel. I hung up the phone and dialed Tracie's number again. "Your call is being routed to T-Mobile." I let out a growl and chucked my phone to the back seat with the clicker. Click, Click, Click. "What the hell was going on?" I thought to myself. I know damn well that the phone bills were paid. Remembering my second phone, I grabbed it from the glove compartment. As soon as it came on, before I could even get to my contact list, 40 different text messages and missed calls started to pop up. One of the ones that stood out that made my stomach turn notes, "Code Black, Call me, MO, read the message from my publicist. "Fuck, there is no way, Code Black, no way," I said, still clicking off messages so I could call Tracie to let me through the gate. Before I could hit dial, the gate opened with two big muscles, Dwayne The Rock looking dudes, coming out and waving for the paparazzi to get out of the way and waving at me to pull through the gate. Click, click, cilantro; the camera kept going off. I pulled the car into my roundabout. My heart dropped, thinking something had happened to Tracie or the twins. As I put the car in park, the gate was closing. My car door was opened by one of the dudes. "Mr. Williams, this way," he said. "Nigga I know the way; this is my damn house," I said, getting irritated. "And who the fuck are you," I said, walking up to my front door about to open it, but it was opened by another guy dressed in all black that I didn't recognize. Wtf is going on. ... I walked into the foyer, looking into the living room, I saw Tracie, her mom, two men dressed in suits that I didn't recognize. "T, I am so glad you're ok," walking towards her, but I was stopped by one of the security guards from outside. "Please, Mr. Damon, step back," grabbing my arm. "Nigga let go of me; this is my damn house," I said, pulling out of his reach. "Tracie, what the fuck is going on? Why are all these people and media here?" I said, looking dead at her. She looked like she had been crying for hours; she moved closed to her mom on the couch and diverted my gaze. She started crying. "Mr. Damon," one of the two men I didn't recognize said, stepping towards me. "Do you know a Janice Neal?" Still focused on Tracie and why she was crying, "No, why?" I tried stepping towards Tracie again; this time, the other guy in a suit blocked my way. "Mr. Damon, my name is Detective Johnson; we need you to come with us down to the station; we have some questions for you." "What questions? I am not going anywhere til someone tells me why the fuck my wife is crying," I said, trying to get around him to get to Tracie. "Tracie, why are you crying, baby? What is this all about? Where are the boys?" I yelled, getting pissed. "Sir, I need you to calm down, Detective Johnson said, "No need to yell." "Man, I was talking to my wife not to you or anyone else," I said, pushing past him. His partner grabbed my arm and pulled it behind me. I tried to pull out from him, but then out of nowhere, two uniform officers appeared and pushed me to the floor and slapped on handcuffs.

I started to really panic and yell, "Tracie, what the fuck, baby, help me, what is going on?" "Mr. Damon, please calm down, don't make this harder than it needs to be," Detective Johnson said calmly as the officers pulled me from the floor and stood me up. Tracie began to sob harder and louder. Her mom said, "Can you please get him out of here? My daughter has been through enough." "Wait, Ok, can you please tell me why the fuck I am in handcuffs? Shit," I said, still yelling, as they moved me towards the front door. Fuck the media; I thought as the front door opened. Click, Click, Click, the media cameras went off. The cop car was parked outside the gate, which was already opened. As we walked to the cop car, the paparazzi yelled, "Markus, Markus, is it true you are the leader of a sex traffic ring?" "Did you rape a 16-year-old girl?" My head started to swirl; the blood rushed to my head as the cops pushed me into the backseat of the cop car. I know I didn't just hear that shit; how the fuck. "Code Black, Code Black," the text from Mo, my publicist, screamed in my head. Click, Click, Click; the flashing from the camera made me close my eyes. "How the fuck did they find out about the sex ring," I said out loud. Before the car pulled off, I looked out the window back up to the house and saw Tracie standing in the doorway. If I didn't know any better, I swear I saw my wife smirking and even almost gloating. "No way," I said to myself, thinking how the fuck I was going to get out of this hell.

The day had gone by so quickly, from landing on a private jet, checking into a penthouse at the Downtown Hilton New Orleans to now waiting in a private green room at the Dome, waiting for him to go on stage. We had spent most of the day shopping and at different museums in the French quarter, hand in hand. This was too good to be true, it seemed, and then I was brought back to earth when I got morning sickness after smelling all the food at the French quarter market. It took everything I had to keep me from puking all over Durrell. "R&B Mogul Markus Damon has been taken into question by the Dallas Police Department after the discovery of a sex ring scheme, including other top executives. More tonight at 10 pm," the reporter on the TV in the room I was in reported. That's what snapped me out of my thoughts, and I looked at the screen. "What in the holy hell was going on," I thought to myself. Markus and a sex ring, in custody. I had no clue what was going on with that, but I had a big situation to deal with. I needed to tell Durrell about this baby before things got too far on. I turned the TV off and turned my attention outside the glass window that looked out over the auditorium; there he was, center stage with his band completing his mic check. I had to tell him, but I didn't want to do it before such a big performance. He was going to need to be focused, and news like this would throw anyone off. Especially how this all started. Another wave of nausea came over me. Just thinking about how this conversation was going to go down, it was so strong that it made me feel like I was going to faint. The door to the suite opened and a white lady with a bucket of champagne entered. "Mr. Babbs, this is for you to enjoy," she said, placing the bucket on one of the tables. The smell of her perfume was so loud that I thought I was going to puke right on the floor. I needed to get some fresh air. "Excuse me, can you let Mr. Babbs know that I am not feeling well and that I will be back in time for his set?" I said to the lady as I walked out of the suite. I decided to head back to the penthouse to lay down for just a few and come back since it was few hours before he performed. After he is done performing, I will tell him. I had to tell him. Rubbing my belly as I walked, "I promise you, baby, we will tell your Daddy soon as he is off stage.

Soundcheck took two hours longer than it should have. All I wanted to do was get back to Meshia and breathe in her scent. As I walk into my dressing room, I saw Nichole, "How and what the fuck are you doing in my dressing room Nichole," I said as I walked in from the soundcheck. I was getting ready for my show at Essence Festival at the Megadome in New Orleans. She was sitting on my loved seat drinking a glass of orange juice, which was strange cause Nikki always drank champagne. "I asked you a question," I said in a stern voice to her. Getting ready to walk back out the door, "Security," I started yelling before Nichole interrupted me. "I wouldn't do that if I were you. You would live to regret that," Nichole said in a matter-of-fact voice. Something about the way she said "live to regret that" made me turn around and stare at her. "You have 5 minutes, and then after that, if you're not gone, I am going to have security throw you out." "Oh, baby, now is that any way to talk to your future?" Nichole said, getting up from the couch and heading towards me. I quickly crossed the room before she could get to me and sat in my chair that read "The general." "Nicky, four and half minutes now," I said. "Okay, once you see what is in this envelope, I bet you will change your tune," she said as she walked back over to the couch and pulled out a manila envelope from her Chanel purse, I had purchased for her this past valentine's day on a trip to Milan. "I wanted to be the one to give you this," Nicky said as she handed me the envelope and went back to the couch, picking her glass back up and putting her feet up. "Don't get comfortable," I said as I looked at the envelope. Just as I began to open up the envelope, my phone began to ring the first verse of "One Last Cry." I immediately reached for the phone, knowing it was Meshia. "Uh, I wouldn't answer that until after you open up that envelope," Nichole said icily as I stared at her through the dressing room mirror. I let the verse play out until my voicemail dinging telling me Meshia left me a message. As I opened the envelope, I took a deep breath and tried to calm my shaking hands. "Why was I so nervous? What could possibly be so important in this damn envelope?" I thought to myself. When I looked down at the photos and the breath I had been holding in, I let it out in surprise. It took a few seconds for my mind to catch up to what I actually saw in the photos. By the second photo, my heart completely broke into pieces when I realized that it was Meshia sucking some dudes dick. When I looked closer and realized that it was Markus, I didn't know whether to let the tears fall or to yell out in anger and hurt. All I could do was to keep going through the photos, which seemed to be over 50 pictures of both of them, in various sexual positions in different places. I felt Nikki's hand on the back of my neck, and I quickly turned, yelling, "Where the hell did you get these? And don't bull shit me, Nichole," as I pushed her hand off me. "A trusted source. I told you that hood rat was no good, but you didn't want to listen to me; that bitch shouldn't have ever been trusted," Nichole said, stepping forward to put her hand back on my neck. Her touch felt like nails being drilled into my skin. I just stared at her and then back at the photos. Nichole said, "So you have two choices, propose to me on stage tonight, or I release these photos to the media, and given the fact that Markus is currently in police custody and probably singing like a canary about the ins and outs of the sex ring, which looks like your little Meshia was a part of, I am sure they will love these photos." I looked at Nichole in question, "What the fuck are you talking about?" "Oh, you don't know, do you?" She said with a chuckle. "Yes, he and few other executives from your label were taken today after someone leaked to the media some photos," she laughed even harder. With every sound of her laugh, my anger raged up. This was bad, really bad. Markus and the sex ring had been outed. Shit, I hope that nigga kept his mouth shut. What the fuck was I going to do? How was Meshia involved with the sex ring? I mean, from the pictures, I can only imagine, but it didn't matter to me because I loved her and had to protect her. I felt like I was going to be sick. I tried to get up from my seat, but Nichole pushed me back down. "Move, Nichole," I said in a dangerous whisper. "NO," she said. "I stood by while you had your little fun with that little hoe, acting like she was better than me. Now it is time to get back to reality. I showed you this for us; I showed you this because we are going to be a family?" She was not shouting louder than need be. "Knock, knock, boss, you, okay?" My head Security, Val, said through the door. "Yes, yes, Val, I'll be out in a second." My head started to spin as I got up and pushed her out of the way so that I could walk over to the couch and grabbed water off the table. Nichole followed behind me and sat next to me. "Did you hear what I said?" I looked up at her, staring her in the face. "What no, what did you say?" As I took a gulp of the water. "I said I did this for our "family," she said as she reached out her purse and pulled out a stack of papers. She handed them to me and looked at me like she was about to cry. "Fuck, what now,

Nikki," I said as I took the papers and looked down. On the papers I looked over, I saw charts and blood test results, and what I read about midway through the page said "6 weeks and 4 days" with a picture of a sonogram attached to it. I jumped from the couch and threw the papers out my even more shaking hands. "What, what, how? Wait, are you saying what I think?" I said to her quietly as the room began to spin harder. I tried to focus on her. "Yes, D, I am pregnant, and it's yours," Nichole said as she placed her hand over her stomach. I ran over to the trash can and threw up the water I had just drunk. "I, I, I," was all I could say as I wiped my mouth with the back of my shirt and sat back down. "Look, D, I know I just dropped a shit load on you, and before your performance. I just felt like these were two things you needed to know, but this is something we have always wanted, right, a family. You, me, and our little baby," she said, taking my hand and placing it over her stomach. I wanted to pull my hand away, but something made me leave it there. Finding out Meshia had fucked Markus was one thing, but to see it in those photos was like taking a dagger straight through my heart. "D, say something," Nichole said, interrupting my thought. I looked back at her in her eyes and said the only thing someone could say in my position. "A baby?" I said with tears falling from my eyes. Nichole took my face in her hands, "Our baby." "Knock, knock. Twenty minutes til stage time, boss," Val said from the other side of the door, as Nichole took my face into her hands, saying, "No D, "our" baby." I knew at that moment that I was fucked. If I didn't marry Nichole, I was going to lose everything; Meshia was going to lose everything. Even seeing Meshia with Markus in those pictures, my love had not changed. For now, I had no choice but to follow through with marrying Nichole, at least make it appear that way until I found a way to neutralize her and make sure the baby, she was carrying was actually mine. This shit was going to hurt Meshia, but it was the best thing I could do to protect her. "It's showtime, Boss," Val said through the door again, "Fuck, let's get this shit over with," I said to Nichole as I got up from my chair and headed for the door. Shit, this just turned into the worse night of my life.

NICHOLE

OMG, I couldn't have planned a better outcome for "the plan." Shit, had I known all I had to do was actually get pregnant and blackmail him, I wouldn't have wasted all my time trying to secure his sperm in a container bull shit. Thanks to Tracie and her little media leak about the sex ring information I had found when I went snooping at Markus Condo. This was turning out to be a win for me all the way around. I didn't have a plan of the marriage thing until I saw on the news that Markus was in custody. I figured I had to think quickly on my feet to get Durrell to listen to me about the baby. I mean, at the end of the day, I was pregnant. How I got pregnant didn't need to be told as it was still Durrell's baby. "I should have used blackmail a long ass time ago," I said as I stared down at the enormous 15-carat ring D had placed on my hand live on stage. Yas!!!!! I wanted to scream out, but I had to keep my composure. I was waiting off to the side for the show to end. So what? The ring was meant for that hood rat. It didn't matter now. Payback is a bitch, and from the moment I found out that Markus was fucking Meshia behind my back. Yeah, I know that he is married to my best friend, but I met Markus long before Tracie even existed. The fact he chose to wife her ass over me was the first blow, and then I saw him and Meshia outside the client a few months back. Shit, he wouldn't even go with me to my appointment that same day. He told me that he had more important things to do than to sit at an abortion clinic with me as they sucked our baby. Well, then, what the fuck made that bitch so special? Over the years, I had grown accustomed to my position in Markus's life as he played house with wifey. I was there in the shadows; I went on every trip he ever took her on. He made sure my bills were paid. He even paid for my college degree. But all that changed when Markus started managing Durrell. At first, dating Durrell was just to make Markus mad. I had no intentions of staying with him, but when Markus didn't even react when he found out, I figured, shit, why not keep Durrell? His career was taking off, the dick was a phenomenon, and he treated me like wifey. It wasn't until Markus walked in on Durrell and me having sex, which of course I planned for him to walk in, that he started to call me again, and we started fucking again, which is how I ended up at the damn clinic the day I found out about Meshia. When I was lying on that clinic table watching them suck my baby from my body, that's when I vowed that one way or another, I would make Markus regret the day he ever left me. "All of them deserve this; they all hurt you," the voice in my head said to me. Brrttt Brttt. The feel of my phone vibrating in the back pocket of my Chanel Jeans brought me back to reality. I grabbed my phone and punched in my code to see a text message from D. "The announcement aired, and the photos delivered." I smiled even harder as I texted back, "My day gets better and better." I snapped a picture of my ring and hit send. Brtt Btrrr. "DOC," replying, "I guess I should say congratulations." I replied, "Don't be an ass; we are both going to get everything we ever wanted. Text me when it is done." Just as I hit send and slid the phone back into my back pocket, I looked up to the stage and saw Durrell wave at me as he sang the last verse of Brian

McKnight's "One last cry." I beamed at him and rubbed my belly and waved backed. It won't be hard to fake this pregnancy. It's way easier when your brother is a Doctor; I laughed to myself as I danced to my "baby daddy's" voice.

MESHIA

I couldn't believe that what I was watching; he was getting married. Durrell was standing on stage at Essence Festival at the Dome in New Orleans, proposing to that blonde fake bitch. I couldn't believe this as I turned the volume up because I couldn't hear what was happening on Live TV. "Nichole, you have been there for me in times when no one else understood me," Durrell said as he got on one knee and pulled out a black box from behind his back. Nichole began jumping up and down with a big goofy grin on her face while the audience cheered loudly. Durrell continued ... "I never thought in a million years that I could find...." Click. I turned the TV off and ran to my bathroom with tears streaming down my face.

I felt so sick to my stomach that I had trusted him. That I actually let myself open up to him. I had believed him. What we shared was although brief, but I believed him. "Shit, this is why he didn't answer the phone when I called." I called him when I woke up from my nap to let him know I was on my way back. I couldn't stop crying as I leaned over the toilet bowl and watched everything, I had for breakfast come out. After throwing up for what seemed like forever, "How the Fuck did I get myself in this shit again? Why is it that love just seems to keep kicking me in my face? Shit, why do I keep putting myself through this shit?" After crying and lying on the bathroom floor for what seemed like hours, I got up, turned on the shower to the hottest level setting, stripped naked, and got in. I grabbed my loofah and body washed and allowed the hot water to cover my skin. The water was so hot that it felt like fire when it touched my skin, but it wasn't as painful as the emptiness I felt in my heart. The tears started to stream down my face. I took my loofah and tried to wash away every touch Durrell had placed on my body. "How could he do this to me? Didn't anything we shared mean anything? I guess not. I guess blonde-headed bitches are more suitable to his lifestyle. I had washed my skin for so hard and long that the water had run cold. I turned off the shower and stepped out, wrapping a towel around my body. I walked over to the corner where the pregnancy test had landed and picked it up; I looked at it and then at my reflection several times. I placed my hand over my stomach, looked back at myself, and saw what a mess I was. "I promise you this little one," I said as I rubbed my flat stomach in a circular motion, "I won't let anyone ever hurt you, and I will make him pay! I promise you that." I looked back at my reflection, trying to picture myself with a swollen belly on my small frame. I said out loud, "I don't know how this is going to play out, but I do know that this time, I am keeping my baby."

To be Continued

For the Love of it All 2

Me. Myself. I.

MONIKA WILLIAMSON grew up in Colorado and has family roots from Alabama and South Carolina. She began writing poetry and short stories at the age of 10. Her creativity continued with discovering a passion for acting and crafting. Monika's friends and family lovingly refer to her as "The Black Martha Stewart" because of her business acumen and her creativity. Monika Denise is a mother of two incredible children: a son and a daughter. She graduated from Our Lady of the Lake University. She owns Black Silk Inc., which is a multi-service communications and craft consulting firm located in Katy, Texas. Also, she is the host of The Tea with Mo internet radio show. Ms. Mo is an entertainment powerhouse with a great work ethic that has been the driving force behind her extraordinary success.